STRANGE
EVENTS
EVEN FOR AN
APOCALYPSE

JAMIE HORWATH

authorHOUSE®

AuthorHouse™
1663 Liberty Drive
Bloomington, IN 47403
www.authorhouse.com
Phone: 1 (800) 839-8640

Published by AuthorHouse 12/11/2018

ISBN: 978-1-5462-7199-4 (sc)
ISBN: 978-1-5462-7201-4 (hc)
ISBN: 978-1-5462-7200-7 (e)

Library of Congress Control Number: 2018914650

Print information available on the last page.

CONTENTS

THE VOID

H mm, where to begin? The easiest way to make sense of it all is to go all the way back to before existence. I would say before time, but I've always been here, documenting everything from the smallest breath to the largest lie. In the very beginning, nothing existed but a never-ending black void. I sat and watched for eons until the tiniest bits of energy seeped into the nothingness. Although small at first, the energy began to grow until twelve beings formed. These beings were known as Eternals—six males formed of darkness and six females formed of light. The Eternals formed a council of twelve and separated the void into six planes. A dark and light being oversaw each plane. The story really begins with a simple betrayal—or what some might say was a lover's spat.

Every so often the Eternals would convene at a council and share their thoughts and ideas. The two Eternals paired to oversee each plane were life partners—a marriage, so to speak, in the broadest sense of the term. A problem surfaced when Learyana and Gemsheer began a romance in secret. The affair went on for eons without notice until Denod, Learyana's husband, found something amiss. At first Learyana became disinterested in Denod. Her touch lost its warmth, and her embrace became callous. Over time Denod noticed how Learyana fawned over Gemsheer during the council meetings, and one night he confirmed his suspicions.

Denod stood in the doorway and watched Learyana and Gemsheer share the touch of lovers in his own bed. His tall, brooding figure cast no shadow in the light provided by the aura of Learyana. His face held two red eyes, watching the lovers exchange passionate kisses, and his thick, razor-clawed fingers clenched into fists. Denod arched his back,

1

emphasizing his broad shoulders. Two horns protruded from his bald head, which sat atop his ten-foot-tall frame. Denod stepped through the doorway.

"Betrayers!" screamed Denod, moving quickly and tossing Gemsheer across the room.

"Denod!" screamed Learyana. "Denod!"

Gemsheer crashed against the rock wall of the bedroom and didn't move. Denod walked over to his prone body and picked him up by the neck, his powerful arm showing no hesitation in hoisting Gemsheer in the air.

Denod looked at his fellow Eternal with contempt and slowly cut Gemsheer's cheek with his razor-sharp claw. Learyana ran to Denod and tried to overpower him, but her slight form could do nothing against Denod's rocklike stature.

Gemsheer gasped for air as Denod's grip around his throat tightened.

"Never did I think you would betray me, brother," said Denod.

"Stop, Denod!" cried Learyana. "It's not his fault."

"Silence!" shouted Denod.

Gemsheer tried to struggle, but Denod held him fast with an authoritative grasp and slowly dragged him to the far corner of the room. Using his free hand to produce a blue aura that opened a door in the wall, Denod shouted, "I cast you into the void, adulterer!"

"No, Denod," mumbled Gemsheer.

Denod pulled back his hand and punched Gemsheer in the stomach. Razorlike claws ripped through Gemsheer's flesh and exposed his insides to the cold surroundings. The Eternal's body grew limp, and Denod shoved the lifeless husk into the void. Learyana ran to the door, but Denod grabbed her long, flowing white hair and yanked her down on her knees.

"I have something special planned for you, my love," he said.

Learyana watched Gemsheer's lifeless body float into the void, his blood and organs spilling out of his stomach into the unforgiving nothingness of the black. Denod grabbed Learyana, tossed her over his shoulder, and walked out of the bedroom. Learyana cried over her lost love and pounded on Denod's cold black skin. She continued to weep until her tears gave way to unconsciousness. Denod carried her through winding catacombs for hours until he finally reached his destination. He dropped Learyana on the cold floor of a barren room and stepped back.

"I will keep you for eternity in a prison, my dear," said Denod as he placed his hands on the floor in front of Learyana. A translucent light rose from the floor and encased Learyana. The prison took the shape of a large sphere that floated inches off the ground.

Denod looked at Learyana with disgust and slowly walked into the depths of the catacombs, alone with his twisted thoughts.

Unbeknown to Denod, something began to happen in the void.

Gemsheer's lifeblood flowed into the blackness until it had completely drained from his body. The blood floated through the endless black, separating into individual cells, which scattered into the endless space of the void. Tiny sparks of energy crackled from the cells, and life began to take shape. Gemsheer's lifeblood was integrated into every corner of the void, and out of death, life grew.

Denod walked the depths of the dark catacombs for years on end, his thoughts becoming corrupted over time until he gently fell into madness. Fearful of retribution from the Eternal council, he closed off his plane from their reach and sat alone in the darkness. Every so often, he would peer into the void and notice the life that had begun to grow. He wondered what kind of life existed, and malevolent thoughts began to creep into his mind.

"A world to rule," mumbled Denod. "How fitting. A world crafted out of malice and hatred born by darkness."

Denod grew bored watching and stepped into the void. He would bring his atrocities to the innocents who infested his domain until he made every form of life feel his betrayal and pain.

* * * *

John Brightman found himself alone in the blackness. Machinery ground in the background, interrupting his thoughts. Dark images, blacker than his surroundings, haunted him. The macabre pictures presented themselves in ever-changing forms that mocked him and tormented his sanity. Winged creatures with inhuman appendages dived near his head. Their claws grazed his face and shoulders as they tried to see how close they could get. The sound of machinery intensified, drowning out the never-ending hissing of his harassers. Gears ground, and metal screeched on metal, sending sharp pain through his mind. John's vision began to blur from the nonstop attack on his eardrums. He stumbled through the blackness aimlessly.

Groups of red eyes would appear every so often, stalking him and watching his every breath. Their gaze did not stay long; something bigger, hidden behind a black curtain of loss, scattered them away. John could sense it. The floor grew wet and soft as he slowly trudged on. The air around him turned cold, and the hairs on his naked body stood on end. Hopelessness filled his mind, and he fell to the darkness. John's legs gave out, and he curled into the fetal position on the wet ground. Pairs of red eyes began to appear around him and slowly inched closer. In the distance something began slithering toward him. He couldn't discern what it was. A sound pierced his ears, and terror began to fill his mind. *Just get up*, he thought. But a deep paralysis crept over his body and kept him from moving as the slithering sound drew closer.

"Brightman," said a soft female voice. "John."

The voice broke through the grinding machinery, and John's thoughts became clearer. He could feel his muscles regain movement. The ever-watching red eyes blinked and scattered from his view. The slithering sound, which couldn't have been more than a few feet away, withdrew into the blackness. John slowly stood up, and a faint white light broke through the dark. The light may have been insignificant within the sea of nothingness, but it gave John hope and enough will to continue moving through his hell.

"John," said the female voice again. It sounded familiar to him. Perhaps it was a memory or a hallucination from a better time.

In the distance John could see a tiny ball of light that shined like a beacon, cutting through the dark. That was when he heard a sound not in alignment with the surroundings. It was very faint but discernible, even through the screeching of metal and gears. The gentle sound of wings flapping entered his ears, and a silhouette of a bird crossed his eye, made visible by the light in the distance. Brightman couldn't tell what type of bird it was or why one would even be here in this black pit of hell. The light began to creep in overhead, sending comfort to his mind. The red eyes remained on his sides, but they kept away from the light. The air around John felt warmer, and the ground became firm, providing a solid base for his steps. His bare feet began to gain traction, and as a result, the speed of his gait increased.

"Brightman." The female voice echoed in his ears.

John's thoughts grew cloudy for a moment, and then a pain shot into his head. He grasped his temples and turned in a circle with both hands covering his ears. A series of pictures sped uncontrollably through his mind—so fast that he could not discern what they were or where they came from. He heard thoughts and conversations from other people. Memories of events that he had never experienced flashed in front of him. The visions began to slow, and images of bits of computer circuitry replaced the wash of memories. The bright colors from the collage of scenes dissipated, replaced by lines and nodes of white. Stars began to appear, and planets with bright moons ran through his mind. Cries filled his ears. A feeling of despair broke into his consciousness. John felt great loss and pain, almost as if he was experiencing the cries of mass genocide. Overwhelmed, he collapsed onto his back and was unable to move.

A vision began to form and overtook his sight. The blackness disappeared, and a rocky landscape surrounded him. On the horizon John could see what appeared to be a dam. On his right side, a blue jay sat atop a rock formation. It chirped once at John and then flew toward the dam, its wings cutting through the breeze with ease. The blue jay disappeared, and the landscape of the sunbaked rocks slowly faded back to the sullen blackness that forever haunted John.

"Brightman, are you awake?" asked the female voice.

The tone pleased Brightman, and he could feel his mind calming.

A few feet in front of John a large white door appeared. The door gave off a radiance that was inviting. John slowly rose to his feet and walked toward the door. He looked back and knew the intrusive sounds of machinery and peering eyes would be waiting for him in the blackness. It let him go for now, plotting and planning for the next time Brightman would be here, if such a thing as blackness could have thought. This, this was something more, though. Something within the dark lived and breathed, waiting only for John's return.

Turning his thoughts away from the blackness, John walked through the door. Light surrounded him. His body began to break down and re-form. Out of the corner of his eye he noticed a fox and bear sitting behind him, almost as if they were guarding him.

Brightman opened his eyes to the sight of Ashley peering over him. She had her hands on her hips and looked into his eyes. John noticed the fading sunlight highlighting her auburn hair. A pair of goggles sat around her neck, and her black jumpsuit barely hid the curves of her body. A large black duffel bag lay near her feet. She sat down next to John and reached into her pocket.

"Eat this," said Ashley. "You slept the day away. We still have maybe an hour of light left, so it's time to get moving. The creatures will be coming back."

John pushed away the light blanket that covered him and noticed he had clothes on: a pair of ripped dirty blue jeans and a gray T-shirt. He took a small pill and a brown cube from Ashley and quickly ate them.

"I found clothes and dressed you," said Ashley. "Here, these might fit."

John looked at Ashley curiously and put on the pair of boots she gave him. "I don't usually have women dress me. Just so you know," he said, lacing up the brown work boots.

"Nothing I haven't seen before," said Ashley.

"That's not what most of my girlfriends say," said Brightman, smiling.

Ashley rolled her eyes and stood up quickly. She grabbed the duffel bag and tossed it across her shoulder, quickly grabbing a flame unit out of it in the process. "Look, I'm not your girlfriend. I'm here to find you and get you back to the elders. I've completed half of my job. Apparently you're important to those guys, so I'm doing what I'm told. Besides, what I saw wasn't that impressive."

Brightman slowly stood up and stretched. His back cracked slightly. He reached up and rubbed his head and noticed he was bald. "What happened to my hair?"

"Side effect of being in a fluid mask. Look, you're lucky to be alive. You were in gestation, and if I hadn't found you when I did, you'd be in the stomach of some very nasty creatures. The rest of you would be floating in that shit in the house I found you in," said Ashley in a serious tone. "We don't have time to talk. Follow me and do what I say. We're heading north for now. My extraction pod isn't far. The sooner we get back underground, the better."

"Uh, yeah, you're going to have to fill me in on some things," said John. "Like what the hell is going on, and what the hell is with all this?" He paused and looked around at the surroundings. The sky held some sort of strange reddish-purplish hue, and the ground sprouted patches of a bizarre red substance, which seemed to be alive, that he had never seen before. A strange growth covered the surrounding buildings, and bones littered the ground along with some indiscernible humanlike growths. "Where are we? The last thing I remember is waking up from a night out clubbing, and then the world turns to shit. I think I deserve an explanation."

Ashley ignored him and started walking forward.

"Hey!" said Brightman, "you said that I was important. Well, if you don't tell me what's going on, I'm not moving."

Ashley turned around and raised her voice. "You can talk and walk at the same time, can't you?"

"Yeah, sure," said John.

"Well, follow me and I'll try to explain what I can," said Ashley, her tone calming a bit.

Brightman began walking forward behind Ashley, and the two progressed slowly to the north in the last bit of the fading sunlight.

"So what's with all the destruction and death?" asked Brightman.

"You really don't know, do you?" asked Ashley.

Brightman shook his head and sighed. "No."

"Fine. An attack from an unknown enemy took humanity by surprise. People think it was an army fuckup or something, but nobody really knows. These creatures were able to hide among us, and they infiltrated us. Slowly, they began to pick us off one by one, and they assumed positions of power. The creatures took many forms and are smart. They can build things, and they know us better than we know them. Some scientist discovered them by accident. Of course, nobody believed him until it was too late. A big war started. It wasn't a conventional war that is in the history books. This war delved into more genetics than anything and became known as the Flesh Wars. So humanity decided to escape underground in big ships. I wasn't alive during this time. Some of the people made it, but most died—"

"Burrowed underground," interrupted Brightman.

"Yep," said Ashley. "Scientists found a place to hide from the creatures until they could figure out how to stop them. Their first attempt failed miserably. That's pretty much why the sky is all these funky colors. The next plan was The Observers."

"Observers?" asked John.

"Yeah, that would be you," said Ashley. "You are the last one. Apparently you have a tape recorder in your head, and the scientists hope you recorded something that they can use."

"Wait, what?" asked Brightman. "I have a recording device in my head?"

"That's what I said, didn't I," said Ashley.

"Well, how are they going to get it out?" asked John.

Ashley began to speak, and then stopped and put her arm out to halt Brightman's walk. She motioned to him, and the two quietly took cover behind a rusted car frame. "Don't move or speak," whispered Ashley.

Brightman and Ashley placed their backs against the remains of the old car. The sunlight began to fade fast, and the ground started to shake. The vibrations started small at first and grew stronger. In the distance a large mass became visible. As the creature drew closer, six large brown legs with spiked claws at the end embedded themselves into the ground. Each time a leg struck the earth, the ground rattled. Long legs covered in reddish hair extended from a large brown body. The underbelly was transparent and seemed to contain faces of the creature's victims floating in a see-through substance. The head of the creature had two large black eyes and a set of mandibles that looked like they could cut through steel, let alone a human body. On the back of the spiderlike form a large brown bulb with six tentacles sprouting from the butt weaved through the air. The tentacles had mouths lined with sharp teeth at the end with spear like tongues that would poke forth. The tongues tested the surroundings around the creature.

"Don't move," whispered Ashley. "Don't even breathe."

Brightman gave her a sideways glance and covered his mouth. He was in awe of the giant creature in front of him. The spiderlike monstrosity moved at a slow pace and paused when it drew even with the rusted car. The tentacles on the back searched for their prey, and one began to sneak around toward Ashley and John.

"Shit," mumbled Ashley. "Grab my hand."

John looked at her, and then quickly grasped her hand.

Ashley bumped the tiny watch on her arm. "Don't let go, whatever you do!" she shouted.

The creature roared on its back legs and turned to look at the car. The tentacles writhed in the air, waving against the reddish-purple sky. The mouths hissed as the tongues protruded forth. A bright light encased Ashley and Brightman. The light filtered through the colors of the spectrum, and time began to lose meaning. Ashley grabbed a flare gun from her duffel bag and shot it toward the house she had found Brightman in. Moving faster than John had ever seen her, she pulled him with her, and the two ran away from the giant spiderlike creature toward a dilapidated house. The surrounding area blurred, and the audible cries of the creature became lost in time. In a blink Ashley and John were inside a small house and the creature was gone. The light around them began to fade, and time returned to normal. Ashley put on her goggles and scanned the area. The spider moved into the distance and began to destroy the remnants of the house she had found Brightman in. Satisfied with its destruction, the giant moved into the barren stretches of the wasteland. Ashley felt a buzzing in her ear and reached to a COMM unit. "Shit," she mumbled as she banged the small COMM on her knee.

"What's wrong?" asked Brightman.

"COMM busted," replied Ashley. "It must have happened in the tachyon pulse."

"Tachyon pulse?" asked John. "What the hell just happened?"

Ashley threw the COMM on the ground and grabbed a black box from the duffel bag. "It's a device that allows you to move faster than light for a short period of time."

"Hey, that's great. So let's just tachyon our way back to the underground," said John.

"It doesn't work like that. There are only a few charges left. Once the charges are depleted, the recharge time is long unless it's hooked up to the mainframe," said Ashley. "Damn it, I shouldn't have wasted that charge earlier."

Ashley walked around the house and checked the door and broken windows. She placed the small black box on the window ledge, and red beams stretched across the inside of the house. "This should cloak us for a while. It's too dangerous to travel at night. The creatures know you were there, so I expect more to be around. We'll move at first light. I suggest you try to get some rest. You're probably in shock, and I don't blame you."

John sat against a moldy wall of the dilapidated house. "Sleep and I don't get along so well," he said.

Ashley peered out the window with her goggles and scanned the area. She detected movement in the distance, very small blips. "Why's that?"

"I've been having bad dreams," muttered John as he rubbed his head.

"Everyone has bad dreams these days," said Ashley as she sat down across from Brightman.

"Not like mine," said John. "It's almost like they aren't dreams, but I'm actually in another place when I sleep."

Ashley unbuttoned a few buttons on her jumpsuit. Her white skin shined in the darkness backlit by the red light. She tied up her long hair in a ponytail and rummaged through her duffel bag. "What kind of place?" she asked. "Has to be better than this."

John didn't answer at first and ran his head over his bald head. "It's usually all black. There are weird sounds, and these peering red eyes follow me everywhere."

"Underground, some people mentioned having nightmares. They called it the Sub Blackness. No one made a big deal about it. Living underground can do strange things to people's minds. Nobody cared, until a few people started disappearing," said Ashley.

"Like vanished?" asked Brightman.

"Maybe," replied Ashley. "Most likely suicides, to be honest. People who couldn't take living like rats. The underground is not a great place, John. Consider yourself lucky to not have been there."

"Well, I must have been down there for some time," said John. "I just don't remember anything. The only thing I really remember is a crazy white light and then you pulling me out of that house. The only things that seem concrete have been what's happened with you. Everything else is just black. Tell me about it, Ashley. I want to know. Tell me about the Sub Blackness."

Ashley crossed her legs and sat Indian-style. She looked at Brightman and studied his features. She quickly pushed away certain thoughts that entered her mind and sat in silence for a moment. "The underground is fragmented. People broke into different groups trying to feel good about themselves by sharing thoughts with those who had like minds. Poverty runs rampant, and freedom is basically an illusion. The elders banned anything pertaining to the old world: books, magazines, newspapers, games, and so on. A small radical sect formed tied to extreme religious beliefs. They started spewing rhetoric about a Sub Blackness. I guess it's their idea of a hell. Most people ignored it until."

"Until …?" said John.

"Until a few months ago when some video footage of a recon agent was discovered," said Ashley. "She was attacked by some sort of shapeless black mist. The sub blackies found out about it, and their rhetoric intensified. This time people listened more. Paranoia began creeping in, and the underground began to split even more than it already was. Rumors started about a civil war from within. There was another thing: a story about three recon agents gone rogue—Bear, Bird, and Fox."

Brightman looked up and paused. "Did you say Bear, Bird, and Fox?"

"Yeah," said Ashley. "Derelict recon party. They're all dead, to my knowledge, and all the way on the West Coast."

John shifted a bit and spoke in a more serious tone. "In my dream— the last one, anyway—I saw a blue jay, a bear, and a fox. Not people, but the animals. The bird flew toward a dam. The thing was, when I was dreaming the blackness left and I saw a rocky area."

"Look, Brightman," said Ashley, "you were just freed from a fluid mask during gestation. Parasites infested your body, and who knows what toxins they pumped into your brain. You're probably just recovering from shock. Try to get some sleep. We have a long journey tomorrow. The quicker we get back to the extraction pod, the sooner this will all be over."

John shrugged and sat back against the moldy wall. He watched Ashley lie down on her side. He looked at her enticing figure, long legs stretched out across a ripped carpet showing all her dangerous curves.

"Don't stare, Brightman," said Ashley. "The red light will camouflage us. Get some sleep."

Brightman shrugged off her last comment, and he lay on his back, staring up at the peeling ceiling. *Easy for you to say*, he thought. Brightman tried to fight off the inevitable sleep, but soon his mind began to leave him, and the blackness returned …

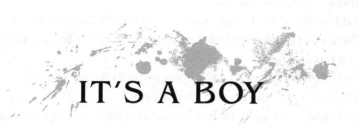

IT'S A BOY

Bird let out a loud scream that filled the makeshift delivery room. Pain coursed through her body and made breathing difficult. She closed her eyes and tried to block out the agony.

"Almost done, Bird," said the doctor. "I just need you to give one more good push."

Bird clenched the white bedsheets and screamed again. Her eyes opened, and she looked up at the ceiling.

"That's it," shouted the doctor. "Look at that. It's a boy!"

Relief filled her mind, and Bird slumped back in the bed and closed her eyes. She wanted to see her son, but fatigue overtook her body, and she drifted into unconsciousness. When she awoke, an old woman stood next to her smiling. She handed Bird her child. The baby looked around in wonderment and settled down in his mother's arms. "He's beautiful," said Bird as she cradled her son. She gently moved a scarlet wrap over the newborn's head and caressed his face. "He has his father's eyes."

"I'll leave you two alone," said the old woman. "If you need anything, I'll be outside."

"Thank you," said Bird.

The radio on Bird's nightstand began to quietly play soothing string music. Bits of white energy flashed in the air near the radio. "I have the perfect name for you," said Bird to her child. "Leaf. Your name will be Leaf."

Bird cradled Leaf in her arms as the music filled the small room. People shuffled by the room in the outer hall. Occasionally someone would peek in. Two men kept the curious away for now, allowing only the doctor to enter.

"We have your room ready," said the doctor. "If you're feeling up to it, you two can get settled in."

"I'd like that," said Bird. "Can you bring the radio for me?"

The doctor smiled and picked up the radio. "Why do you like this thing so much?" he asked.

Bird smiled and asked, "Can you show us to our room?"

"Oh sure," said the doctor. "Follow me."

Bird held Leaf tight to her breast and followed the doctor down the hall and into a larger room with a bed, dresser, small refrigerator, nightstand, and crib. "You can set the radio on the nightstand," she said.

"Right," said the doctor. "Anything else?"

"No, thank you," said Bird.

"All right," replied the doctor. "If you need anything, hit the pager and Angela will come over. She'll be helping you with your baby until you get settled."

Bird smiled at the doctor and watched him slowly walk out the room and gently close the door behind him. She turned to the lone window in the room. The view overlooked the makeshift settlement that she now called home. Sunlight cascaded through the dusty window, offering a modest source of light to the small room. The sun rays penetrated the red and purple clouds and comforted Bird. The rancor of the underground no longer haunted her. Leaf's tiny hand grasped Bird's finger tightly. Bird noticed her reflection out of the corner of her eye in the mirror. She noticed her hair slowly returning to its natural blond color. The radio clicked on again, serenading the mother and newborn with a gentle sound of percussion and strings.

A knock on her door interrupted the music slightly. "Who is it?" asked Bird.

"It's Jessup," said a nervous voice. "Can I come in?"

Bird hesitated a moment. She didn't mind Jessup. He had a crush on her and often ended up being helpful. "That's fine," replied Bird.

Jessup slowly opened the door and nervously entered the room. Jessup had a short stature and short reddish hair that sat atop a narrow head. A stained long-sleeve green shirt adorned his chest, and gray work pants covered his legs and waist. A heavy pair of work boots protected his feet. Jessup wore his clothes a bit baggy to hide his small frame. He looked at Bird quickly and then turned his eyes to the floor. "They want you to attend a meeting tonight," said Jessup. "They think it's important that you bring your child with you to show everyone."

"That's fine, Jessup," said Bird. "I'll be there. Wait, *we* will be there— Leaf and I."

"Is that his name?" asked Jessup.

"Yes," said Bird.

"That's a nice name," said Jessup.

"Thank you," said Bird. "Now if you'll excuse us, I'd like to spend some time with my son."

"Right," said Jessup. "See you tonight."

"Okay," replied Bird.

Jessup stood awkwardly in the doorway, eyes cast down toward his boots. He put his hands in his pockets and finally raised his eyes to look at Bird's face. "Your hair, Bird," he said. "It's blond."

Bird smiled back at Jessup and said, "I'll see you at the meeting. Goodbye, Jessup."

"Oh yeah, right," mumbled Jessup. "See you later."

Jessup waved awkwardly at Bird and quickly left the room. *He's not like your father, Leaf,* thought Bird. She laughed a bit, and then her face grew sullen. Memories of Bear crept into her mind from the place she had worked to bury them. Leaf began to cry. Bird caressed his face and kissed his cheek. She opened her shirt and exposed her breast. "Hungry?" said Bird. She walked over to the window again, and after Leaf finished, she placed him in his crib. Content that Leaf would be all right, Bird crawled into her bed and closed her eyes. She could fight her memories no longer, and thoughts of Bear flooded her mind. Bird began to sob lightly. She reached into her pocket and pulled out the postcard of the beach. The radio softly played violin music that mixed with Bird's sobbing.

Another knock on the door pulled Bird away from memories of her dead lover. She sat up in the bed, wiped away her tears, and said, "Come in."

A tall man wearing black fatigues and boots entered the room. A full beard adorned his face, hiding most of his features. He carried a large lockbox. "I've brought your belongings," he said in a deep voice.

"Thank you," said Bird.

The man set the box down in the corner of the room and walked out, closing the door behind him. Bird noticed his sidearm and shrugged. She didn't know his name but had seen him around the settlement a few times. She tried to keep her distance from as many people as she could. They had taken her in, but she still felt like an outsider. Every so often she could feel contemptuous eyes follow her. Bird walked over to the box and opened the lid. Her light blue-and-white jumpsuit sat neatly folded with her helmet on top of it. A katana rested underneath the jumpsuit along with a small black notebook. Memories of her old life rushed back, and she slowly closed the box. She ran her hand over the top of the box and sat on the edge of the bed. Leaf began crying a little, so Bird walked over to the crib and picked up her son. The child's crying slowed until Leaf began to giggle. His tiny hands grasped at the air, and Bird placed his small hand in hers. "What does this world have in mind for us?" she asked herself. "Do you know the answer, my Leaf?"

Bird noticed tiny white hairs on Leaf's head—a color resembling her hair during the time she was pregnant. She thought back on when her hair had changed color months ago. It was when Bear and Bird found the light. The night of Leaf's conception, in the hotel room. Bird looked into Leaf's eyes. "Yes, indeed, what does this world have planned for us?"

Bird tossed her doubts and fear away as quickly as they had entered her mind. Bear had taught her to pay no heed to fear. *If he had given in to his own fears, things would be different from how they are now*, Bird thought. *Maybe he would still be alive, but at the cost of his thoughts and ideals.* Bird wiped away a tear and decided to get some rest. She had an uneasy feeling about the meeting later. Placing Leaf back in his crib, Bird gave in to sleep.

The radio belted out a loud series of percussion beats, and Bird awoke from her sleep. She noticed Angela in the room attending to Leaf.

"He just needed a quick changing," said Angela.

"Thank you," said Bird. "I'll take him now."

Angela nodded and handed Leaf over to Bird. She opened her shirt for Leaf and secured the scarlet wrap around his tiny body. "The meeting will be starting soon," said Angela. "Would you like me to walk you over?"

"Thank you," said Bird.

"Very well," replied Angela.

Bird followed Angela through the hallways of the complex and entered the main meeting hall. A group of people had already taken their seats. Jessup waved to Bird and directed her to a seat in the front of the room. Bird took her seat next to Devin, one of the leaders of the settlement. He wore black fatigues like the man who had brought the box into Bird's room. Other men dressed similarly watched the doors and windows. They all had sidearms, and some carried rifles. Devin stood up and loudly asked for the chatter to quiet down. After a few minutes of rumbling, the crowd grew silent and Devin began to speak.

"Good evening, everyone. As you may have heard, we've had our first childbirth at the settlement. Bird, whom we found months ago, gave birth to a healthy baby boy. Have you thought of a name, Bird?"

Bird looked at Devin and said lightly, "Leaf. His name is Leaf."

Devin smiled. "Well, everyone give a warm welcome to our newest member."

A round of gentle applause filled the room.

"Any other baby news from anyone else?" asked Devin. "Sometimes these things can be contagious."

The crowd remained silent, until a younger man spoke up. "Well, we haven't had success yet, but that doesn't mean we aren't trying."

A few people laughed. Then an older woman spoke quickly, cutting into the laughter. "Does anyone find it strange that Bird is the only woman to have a child? She comes here from out of nowhere and has a baby. What about everyone else? Everyone has been trying. Look at her hair. It's changed."

The crowd grumbled, but then Devin interjected, "Now, now. There is no need to slight the birth of a child. The doctors have run the tests. Nothing has come back on the status of the water or food supply that would lead to sterility."

"Then why is no one else pregnant?" squawked the old woman. "How can we trust these doctors anyway? They're the ones who got us in this mess!"

The crowd rumbled slightly. "No one knows that for sure," said Devin, his voice growing irritated. "You damn well know that your statement is speculation. Our doctors have cured you when you've been ill, and attended to your wounds. They've run extensive tests on our supplies, and they assure us that nothing is wrong. If there were, we would all be dead. Does anyone have anything else to add that isn't gossip?"

The old woman folded her arms and raised her nose. "Not me," she replied.

"Anyone else?" asked Devin.

The crowd mumbled a bit, but no one replied.

"Good," said Devin. "I would like to turn our attention to the search teams. Tempest, have any reports come back yet from the last excursion?"

The man at the far end cleared his throat and said, "Nothing concrete at this time. We received a broken transmission, but it was very garbled and unclear. I was thinking perhaps Bird could use her helmet to track it or even contact the underground again."

Devin looked at Bird as did the rest of the crowd, waiting for her to answer. Bird fidgeted in her chair and spoke gently. "I ran diagnostics on my helmet some time ago. The COMM unit is malfunctioning. I've not been able to send or receive any messages from the underground. As far as picking up random transmissions, I would need to do some repairs, but I don't think I have the proper tools. If the main chip is damaged, it can't be repaired with what we have available."

"Fair enough," said Devin. "Bird, perhaps meet with Randall to see if you two can get it working again."

Bird nodded and pulled the scarlet wrap over Leaf's eyes. She noticed the old woman in the back staring at her with contempt. Bird watched as she whispered to the man sitting next to her. He nodded and quickly left the room.

"Tempest," said Devin, "keep trying to contact the search team. They may have found something or be in trouble. Has anyone noticed any creature activity around the perimeter?"

"About two weeks ago, we downed one near the western caves," replied a man in the crowd. "Nothing unusual, except the creature had a human leg. We took pictures and then burned the body according to the normal protocol."

"I'd like to see those pictures," said Devin. "As far as the remainder of business, the ration lists are posted, and normal job duties are to be followed. However, the main reason I called this meeting is for celebration. Let's celebrate Leaf!"

The crowd applauded and began conversing. The old woman stood up and walked out of the room.

Devin turned to the man who had brought Bird her equipment. "Post two men outside Bird's room for a few days, just as a precaution."

The man nodded and got up from the table. He motioned to the other men in fatigues, and they left the room.

Devin turned to Bird and said, "Don't let what that woman said bother you. This is a time for celebration."

Bird smiled and replied, "If it's okay, I'm going back to my room. Leaf is tired."

Devin sighed. "I understand."

Jessup followed Bird as she left the room and asked, "Everything okay, Bird?"

Bird smiled at Jessup. "Yes, I just need to rest a bit."

"Okay," he replied, "but if you need anything, I'll be around."

"Thanks," said Bird. "I'll talk to you tomorrow."

Jessup nodded and watched as Bird returned to her quarters and shut the door. He lingered a bit and noticed two large men in black fatigues standing in front of her door. *That's odd*, he thought …

Bird put Leaf in his crib and walked over to the box with her gear. Bird knew there was nothing wrong with her COMM. She had disabled it some time ago. She reached into the front pocket of her jumpsuit that lay in the box. She held a small chip in her hand and picked up the helmet. Bird sat on her bed with her legs crossed and set the helmet in front of her. She looked at the chip and gently placed it in a small slot on the right side of her gear. The front of the visor lit up, and various text and numbers ran across the front as the computer rebooted. "Computer, scan for messages, please," said Bird.

"Hello, Bird," said a soft female computerized voice. "Scanning for messages as requested. Would you like to activate the COMM?"

"No," said Bird, "just scan for messages, please."

"Certainly, scanning now. Three transmissions detected."

"Source and location, please," said Bird.

"Unknown …"

GET YOUR OWN

Brightman began falling, and blackness surrounded him. The familiar feeling began to return. His doubts, fears, and indecision clogged his mind. He slowly descended into the blackness and rested on his back. The sound of machinery began to attack his ears again. Drilling sounds and the echo of metal gates slamming sent his thoughts into a paralysis. Brightman's body remained unresponsive to his attempts to move. Two tiny objects gently struck the side of his face. John glanced down and noticed glowing red dice by his cheek.

"Eight again!" the voice of a small boy said, laughing.

"Ha, you lose," chided a little girl.

"Who is that?" asked the boy as he stood over Brightman.

"That's Mr. B, silly," replied the girl.

"Don't touch our dice, Mr. B!" said the boy as he quickly picked them up.

"Yeah, you have to get your own," said the girl. "These belong to us."

"I don't want your dice? Who are you?" asked Brightman.

"We know who you are, but you don't know us," said the girl.

"I don't know who he is," said the boy.

"I told you, that's the Brightman," replied the girl.

John's dark thoughts slowly began to fade, and he realized he could move again. He slowly propped himself up and looked at the two children curiously. "How do you know who I am?" he asked. "And how did you get here?"

"For a Brightman, he isn't too bright," said the boy, laughing.

"Follow us, Mr. B," said the girl as she ran away with the boy.

John watched the two children disappear into the blackness. He shook his head and thought that to be rather odd. The sound of machinery began again, this time even louder, and the cackle and hiss of the winged creatures returned.

"I'd follow them if I were you," said a woman's voice.

"Who said that?" asked Brightman.

Out of the blackness, a tall brunette appeared with a slight aura about her. A lone red strip of hair dangled amidst the sea of black. "I did," she answered.

"Who are you?" asked Brightman.

"That's not important at the moment," she said.

"I would listen to her if I were you," said a deep masculine voice.

Next to the mysterious woman appeared a tall man with broad shoulders and a muscular body. "You don't have much time," he warned.

"We can't protect you forever," said the woman as she and the man positioned themselves in a defensive stance in front of Brightman. "We can buy you some time, but you should go."

"Go where?" asked Brightman.

"Follow the light," replied the man.

Brightman slowly backed away from the strangers and decided to take their advice. "What are you protecting me from?" he asked before he was out of earshot.

The large man punched into the blackness, and Brightman could hear the winged creatures writhe in pain. The man said, "I'd get going, because we can't hold them back forever."

Brightman turned and decided to head in the direction he thought the children went. He had no idea where they went but at that point he didn't care.

"Over here," said the boy.

Brightman turned and walked to his left, not exactly sure where the voice had come from.

"Not that way, stupid," said the girl. "This way, over here."

"I told you he wasn't too bright," said the boy, laughing.

Brightman changed direction and stumbled through the blackness toward the voices. He wasn't sure how long he walked, but in the distance, he saw a tiny light. John quickened his pace, and the light began to grow brighter.

The two children he had seen earlier were near the light, which came from the red dice. When the boy tossed the dice, the girl laughed again and said, "You lose."

"Hello," said Brightman.

"Mr. B," said the girl, "follow us. Don't look at the eyes, though. Ha ha."

The children ran off again. Brightman followed as closely as he could. The light from the dice guided him through the blackness. Tiny red eyes began to appear on his right and left. John ignored them and kept moving with the light. He began to grow tired, and on the next step he lost his balance and stumbled. The ground gave out underneath him, and his body froze in the air. Dozens of red eyes surrounded him. Brightman tried not to look into their gaze. They drew close until in a blink they were gone. John felt himself falling rapidly. A light began to engulf his body, and the rate at which he descended slowed until his feet touched a cold rock floor.

"He made it," said the boy.

"Mr. B," said the girl, "follow us. We want to show you something."

Brightman ran after the children again. They led him through a maze of catacombs until finally the children stopped. John noticed a woman unlike any he had ever seen sitting in a sphere that floated inches above the ground. Long white hair flowed from her head past her waist. Her skin was powder white along with her eyes and lips. Light strands of clothing clung to her skinny figure that showed long legs and arms, a taut stomach, and an ample bosom. A strange green moss grew around the surface of the sphere.

"Who is that?" asked Brightman. "She's beautiful." John felt drawn to the woman and began to inch closer. He reached out to touch the sphere, but his hand passed through as if he were a ghost.

"That's the white lady," said the girl.

Brightman stepped back and looked at her face. "She looks sad," he said.

"She is sad," said the girl.

The white lady shifted inside the sphere, and tears streamed down her cheeks. She reached into the back of her hair and pulled out a long hairpin.

"What's she doing?" asked Brightman.

The white lady looked up and grasped the hairpin with her slender hand. The pin was long and sharp. Brightman watched in horror as she jammed it into her throat. White blood spurted from her neck and covered her body. The woman's eyes closed, and a bright light began to glow from her stomach. The light grew brighter until it filled the sphere. John noticed the outside of the sphere begin to crack until it shattered, allowing the light to escape throughout the catacombs. It bounced around, heading in various directions until finally disappearing from Brightman's view. In the space occupied by the sphere red dice floated in front of Brightman. He slowly reached out and closed his hand around them.

"I said, get your own," said the girl from behind him as she reached out her small hand.

Brightman placed the dice in her open palm and said, "Get my own dice?"

"No, Mr. B," said the girl, laughing. "Get your own memories."

The catacombs lit up as a bright white flashed again, and a fox and large grizzly bear sat in front of Brightman. They looked at him for a moment longer, and then slowly walked into the endless catacombs. John felt weightless again and began falling. He felt the blackness returning as he crashed into the ground.

"Head to the north," said the gruff voice of the man Brightman had seen earlier.

"You will begin to find the answers you seek," said the woman.

The blackness around Brightman began to fade, and the image of a dam appeared—the same one he had seen earlier. This time he noticed that the water around the facility had turned red—blood red. John saw the blue jay again. She circled high above the dam, chirping wildly. The ground began to shake, and Brightman felt his body breaking apart. His thoughts began to slow down, and the familiar smell of the moldy, dilapidated house filled his nostrils. Brightman opened his eyes and awoke from the dream.

Brightman rubbed his bald head and tried to shake out the residue from the night's sleep. The words from the people filled his head. *Head to the north*, he thought. *How am I supposed to persuade Ashley to believe me? She is probably right about something the creatures put in my body.* John decided to keep his dream to himself for now …

"Sleep well?" asked Ashley.

"As well as I could, considering the circumstances, I guess," replied Brightman.

"That doesn't sound too convincing," said Ashley. "At least you're up early. We have the full day of sunlight ahead of us. My extraction pod isn't that far. We should be able to reach it before nightfall."

"Any luck with the COMM?" asked Brightman.

Ashley shrugged. "Unfortunately not, but that's all right. My pod has a COMM. Once we get to it, I can notify the Elders."

"So that's it then," said John.

"What do you mean?" asked Ashley.

"Your mission will be done?" asked Brightman.

"Correct," replied Ashley.

"What happens then?" asked Brightman.

"When I get you back, I go through a debriefing and my usual R-and-R until the next mission," said Ashley.

"I see," said Brightman. "Maybe when we get back underground, we'll meet up again?"

Ashley paused for a moment and said, "Not likely. Part of my debriefing is a selective mind wipe."

"You don't say," said Brightman. "So they erase your memories?"

"I don't want to get into it," said Ashley, a bit of disgust evident in her tone. "It's a mission. It's a job."

"Will I be erased?" asked Brightman.

"If the debriefing requires it, then yes," said Ashley.

"How do you feel about that?" asked Brightman.

"I'm doing the mission I was assigned," replied Ashley. "No offense, Brightman. Look, we're wasting time. Get your things together and let's get moving."

Brightman watched as Ashley stuffed a few things into her duffel bag. Her actions appeared a bit violent and hostile. "I didn't mean to upset you," he said slowly.

Ashley forcefully closed the duffel bag and put it over her shoulder. She pulled her hair into a ponytail and paused a moment. "You didn't," she said. "You're my mission, and I've never failed a mission. Now let's go."

Brightman sighed and followed Ashley out of the dilapidated house. As he looked up, he noticed her tossing a ration cube and water pill toward him. He deftly caught the items with his right hand.

"Eat up," said Ashley.

"Thanks," said Brightman as he popped the rations into his mouth.

Ashley began to walk faster, and an awkward silence began to grow between the two of them. Brightman decided to speak in an attempt to lighten the mood but thought better of it. He looked into the sky and marveled at the red and purple clouds. Somehow the sun found a way to break through the bizarrely colored clouds. Something bothered Brightman about all this. His lack of memories, the strange dreams, the culture of the underground, and Ashley's debriefing. He shook his head in disgust. *I just met this woman*, he thought. *She isn't ugly, that's for sure, and she did save my life, but what exactly did she save me from?*

Brightman stumbled a bit on a rock formation. As his steps grew heavy, he motioned for Ashley's attention. "I need to rest," he said.

Ashley paused and looked him over. "All right, we can take a few minutes. You might want to sit by that rock over there."

Brightman nodded and walked over to the large rock covered in a red substance and sat down. He watched Ashley as she scanned the area with her goggles. The constructs of the old houses gave way to an open field. Red growth covered the ground, and a few large oak trees in their death throes offered a bit of privacy in an otherwise open field. Long greenish-red vines ran across the ground and clumped together in patches. A road overgrown by bizarre vegetation led John to wonder where they were. Ashley mentioned the West Coast, so that ruled that out. The people in the dream had mentioned heading north, so Brightman deduced that they were in a more southern locale. A gentle breeze began to pick up, lifting the red substance into the air. Brightman began to cough violently.

"Put this on," said Ashley, handing him a gas mask.

Brightman fumbled with the mask for a moment, and then Ashley grabbed it from his hands. She looked briefly into his eyes, and then quickly avoided his stare and fastened the mask over his face. Ashley followed suit and put one on her own face.

"How much stuff do you have in that duffel bag?" asked Brightman.

"Enough to get us home safely," she said as the breeze began to pick up. Red dust filled the air, and visibility became a bit difficult. "It's just a windstorm. It should pass soon. The mask will keep that crap out of your lungs."

"What is it, anyway?" asked Brightman.

"It's dead cells from the creature's skin," said Ashley.

Ashley and Brightman struggled to navigate through the windstorm. The red substance ended up being a nuisance, forcing Brightman to wipe off the gas mask to see. The surroundings grew dark as the red dust clouds blotted out the sun's rays. Brightman thought the scenery to be somber and depressing. He decided to break the silence between the two of them.

"Do you think it's ironic that I have no memories except with you?" asked Brightman.

Ashley didn't answer immediately, but then slowed her walk. "Memories are overrated, if you ask me."

"I guess, but I've never had any, or I can't seem to remember them if I did, so I wouldn't know," said Brightman.

"It's not like I have much to be happy about either," said Ashley. "Why would anyone in this world?"

"I might not be able to remember anything, and I might not have lived through what you did, but I'm awake now," said Brightman.

"You have no idea what's going on," said Ashley. "You are the last Observer, John. If the Elders can't get the information they need from your head, that's it. It's over for everyone. For someone named Brightman, you aren't that bright."

"Why does everyone keep saying that to me?" mumbled Brightman.

"That's the first time I've said it," replied Ashley. "Last time I checked, we were the only two people here."

"Never mind," said Brightman. "I just have a hard time believing that I'm the last hope for humanity. I mean, there could be another way."

"To quote my friend Ed, sure as I shit two times every Tuesday," said Ashley. "So no, I'm not the one who figures this stuff out. I'm a grunt.

I just follow orders. The scientists say you are, so you are. I just follow orders."

"I don't believe that," said John.

Ashley paused for a moment. The wind slowly began to die down, and the swirling red dust dissipated. "Here's what is going to happen. We are going to get to my pod, and I'm taking you back down. The scientists will figure it out, like they always do," she said, raising her voice.

"I had another dream last night," said Brightman.

"Enough with those dreams," said Ashley. "Like I told you, it's probably from the poisons of the creatures."

Brightman took off his gas mask and wiped the sweat from his brow. "How can you be so sure?"

Ashley took the mask from Brightman and placed it back in the duffel bag along with her own. "I'd rather trust in something tangible than in some fairy tale you're concocting."

Silence began to grow again. It filled the air with a heaviness that fed into the hopelessness of the surroundings. "Look at this, Brightman," Ashley muttered. "Look at what's around us. No animals. No people. No nothing but a destroyed world. Let's get moving. We've wasted enough time already."

Brightman looked at the ground and then reluctantly began walking again. *Maybe she's right,* he thought. *I've been alive in this world for only a few days. Not that I wasn't alive before, but I have nothing to fall back on except mysterious visions in my dreams.* John's thoughts emptied, and he continued the long walk. The red substance on the ground began to give way, and the road that he had noticed earlier became clearer. On the horizon, structures became visible.

"Hold on," said Ashley as she scanned the area with her goggles.

"What's wrong?" asked Brightman.

"I picked up some movement. The creatures tend to nest in structures, so there could be trouble up ahead. Follow closely. We're going to go through the structures from the rear."

"Why not just go around?" asked Brightman.

"The area is too open," said Ashley. "If there are creatures ahead, they'll spot us for sure. I don't know what kind are up there, if any. Just follow close and be quiet."

Brightman stayed a step behind Ashley. If nothing else, at least the view was pleasant, he thought as he tried not to stare at her backside. He blinked and thought it better to focus than die because he was staring at her ass.

Ashley and Brightman covered the ground quickly until they found shelter behind an old two-story building. A few fairly well-kept structures formed a small alleyway. Ashley peered around the corner and held up her hand, cueing Brightman to wait.

"Brightman! Yeah, you. Over here, sexy," whispered a soft female voice.

John looked around and saw the figure of a woman slip behind the building. He turned away from Ashley and followed. Her voice sparked a curiosity he had never felt before. He felt a burning in his groin.

"This way. Over here. I've been waiting for you," the voice whispered.

Brightman turned the corner and saw a beautiful brunette with extremely large breasts and wide hips dressed in black lingerie. A corset highlighted the curves of her narrow waist quite nicely. She slowly lowered the strap of her bra to expose her ample breast. "Come here, baby," she cooed.

"It looks okay, Brightman," said Ashley. "Brightman?"

Ashley turned around and couldn't find John. That's when she heard the seductive pulsing of the Fuck Machine. "Oh shit!" she screamed.

In a panic Ashley ran around the corner and saw Brightman walking toward the monstrosity. She dropped her duffel bag and ran toward him, crashing into his body and landing on top of him. Brightman began to struggle and push her away. Ashley saw the look in his eyes and pinned his arms on the ground. The Fuck Machine had him ensnared. She looked up and noticed the demon machine was still not close enough to strike. It was still fishing at this point. "Dammit!" shouted Ashley. "You're probably going to enjoy this more than I will!"

Ashley quickly unzipped Brightman's pants and pulled down his underwear. She undid her belt and slid down her jumpsuit pants and underwear. She took a deep breath and allowed Brightman inside her. John's eyes reflected the mad lust infused by the Fuck Machine. Ashley began grinding her hips at a slow pace and then picked up speed. Brightman struggled to break free.

"Listen to me, Brightman!" screamed Ashley. "Concentrate on me!"

Brightman continued to struggle. His mind became fixated on the image of the lustful brunette now naked and dancing for him. Ashley grabbed her top and ripped it open, exposing her ample breasts. She grabbed Brightman's hands and forced him to grab them. She began riding him faster and arched her back. "Focus on me!" shouted Ashley.

Brightman began to relax, and his hands moved to Ashley's hips. The sky above him seemed to roll away at a fast pace. The red and purple clouds mixed together, and Ashley's body became backlit from the sun's rays. Her white skin shined, and her auburn hair danced wildly around her shoulders. He moaned, and then a rush escaped his brain and the image of the brunette began to fade from his vision. Clarity returned, and he looked up at Ashley in shock. "What are you doing?" asked Brightman.

Ashley collapsed on his chest. Her breathing began to slow, and then she rolled off of his body. The two lay there in the reddish-green grass near the side of the building. John noticed graffiti on the side. Various names and the words *lost hope*. Brightman wasn't sure how long the two of them stayed there. Neither of them made a sound until Ashley got up and walked away from Brightman. She turned her back on him and slowly dressed herself.

"What did you just do?" asked Brightman. "Did you just rape me? Not that I envision that as the kind of rape I worry about. Still, care to explain?"

Ashley refused to look in his direction and kept her back to him. "I just saved your life," she said. "That's what I did."

"Okay, if that's how you want to look at it, I can relate to that," said Brightman. "Next time, give me a bit of notice. Let me at least wine and dine you."

"Dammit, Brightman!" shouted Ashley. "There won't be a next time."

"Hey, that's not fair. You didn't give me notice. I thought I performed fine for basically being raped," said Brightman.

Ashley walked over to Brightman, shoved her goggles in his face, and hit the Zoom button. "Look, you idiot. That is what I saved you from!"

Brightman looked through the goggles and became terrified. A large machine with two dolls resembling humans attached to long arms bobbed about. A large tank in the back of the contraption held bits and pieces of human remains. Tubes ran from the dolls into the tank. Various sharp metal devices meant to eviscerate flesh hid just behind the dolls. "What the hell is that?" he asked.

"That is the Fuck Machine," said Ashley, shuddering. "I'll explain later. Let's get out of here before it comes back."

"How come you didn't just zap it with your flamethrower?" asked Brightman. "Seems like you went a little out of the box."

"Okay, Mr. Know It All guy, who has been in this world for how long now?" barked Ashley, visibly irritated.

Brightman zipped up his pants and gave in. "Fine. Did you at least like it?"

Ashley stared at him coldly and said, "Don't push it."

"Okay, okay," he mumbled, trying to conceal a smile. "After you."

"I barely felt anything at all," said Ashley as she began walking. The two of them didn't speak again for some time.

Brightman thought of Ashley differently now. He had a vague knowledge of past girlfriends, but he couldn't tell if they were real or not. He was certain it had been real with Ashley.

"If I hadn't had sex with you, the machine would've killed you, Brightman," said Ashley, finally breaking the awkward silence. "Look, I need to rest. Can you climb a tree?"

Brightman looked at her and replied, "I suppose so. Why?"

She pointed to a large oak tree on the hill and said, "Because we're going to rest in that tree."

Brightman looked at the tree and shrugged. "All right, you haven't gotten me killed yet. I just want to add that this is a very bizarre world."

Ashley began to climb the tree. "You don't know the half of it."

Brightman followed her as best he could. She definitely had better tree-climbing skills than he did. After a struggle, he made it to a high branch. "This is as high as I go."

Ashley grabbed another branch and gently nestled her thin figure on a large limb. "We should be fine here. Look at this, Brightman."

Brightman looked up, and she handed him her goggles.

31

"Look over that rock formation past the trees," she said.

John looked through the goggles in the direction she had pointed and said, "I don't see anything."

"My ship?" asked Ashley. "Don't you see my ship?"

Brightman mumbled, "The only thing I see … Wait, you mean the thing being ripped apart by those people?"

Ashley grabbed the goggles and said," What the hell! Damn robots! I hate robots!"

"Robots?" asked Brightman. "They have robots?"

"Unfortunately, yes," muttered Ashley. "Hold my goggles."

Ashley handed Brightman her goggles and dived from the tree branch, her arms outstretched and her feet pointed toward the sky. With a quick tap of her watch, a tachyon pulse activated, and she disappeared in the blink of an eye. A tiny spark faded into the horizon, and Brightman could discern a bluish line blazing across the ground. He clicked Zoom on the goggles and watched as the robots burst into flames. Ashley appeared and picked up a large rock, and began beating the robots as they burned. She didn't stop. Brightman watched for a bit longer and then decided to run over to her. He didn't move as quickly as she did. When he finally arrived, she was still beating on the broken pieces of metal with a large rock. Blood dripped from her hands as she bashed the hunks of metal. Brightman couldn't watch anymore and pried the rock from her hands. Ashley could barely hold up her arms, and her hands dripped with her own blood. She collapsed against Brightman's chest. He did his best to comfort her as she began sobbing. The wreckage from the extraction pod painted the picture clearly enough. Their ticket home lay in ruins amidst a pile of metal, wires, and blood. One of the robot heads rolled over and seemed to smile eerily. Brightman kicked it aside, and the glowing blue light from its soulless eyes grew dark.

Brightman looked to the sky and noticed the sun beginning to dip behind a mountain range in the distance. Ashley remained motionless. Her sobbing lessoned a bit, but Brightman realized their situation couldn't be much worse. He grabbed Ashley's duffel bag and tossed it and Ashley over his shoulder, buckling under the weight for a moment before gaining his balance. He remembered the voices from his dream. *Head north*, he thought. Slowly, Brightman carried Ashley away from the wrecked vehicle. His shoulders burned, and his legs began to feel like rubber. He could feel his feet chaff against the inside of the boots. Brightman nudged Ashley once, but her body did not respond. The sun dipped out of view, and John continued to walk until he could not see anymore. He gently set Ashley down and rummaged through her duffel bag. The watch on her wrist cast just enough light for him to be able to see what he was doing.

"Where is it?" he muttered to himself. "There!"

Brightman took the black box Ashley used in the house to put up the red lights. He looked at the contraption in bewilderment. Then something flashed in his head. White nodes and lines filled his vision, similar to what he had experienced in his dream. Brightman began to understand the device. He slid open a compartment and toggled a few settings. Red lights emitted from the box and encircled both of them. The circumference was small but shrouded them in the camouflage the light provided. He put his arm around Ashley and held her close. He would not sleep that night. Instead he would lie awake thinking about what the little girl had said: "Get your own ..."

A pale moon became visible once in a while when the clouds shifted in the sky. The light was faint, but it was enough to allow Brightman to discern a few feet outside of their shelter. The red glow cast a hue over their bodies. Brightman placed his hand over Ashley's heart and focused on the steady beat. It helped him cope with the unnatural silence of the night. Thoughts rolled through Brightman's head, and the same words kept repeating over and over: "Get your own ..."

DARKNESS STIRS
AMONG US

Ed saw the dossier slipped under his door. He didn't want to acknowledge it, but he really had no choice. He still had some R-and-R left from his last excursion on the surface. Losing his friend to the amoeba had hit him hard. Plus, his friend happened to be an Observer, which made it even worse. It wasn't that the man was actually Ed's friend. He felt some sympathy for him. Ed had an assignment, and that particular Observer happened to be his. Ed's particular mission involved an Observer who actually didn't kill himself when he woke up. Unfortunately, the man didn't want to believe what he saw and ended up unknowingly trapped by the creatures. They toyed with him for a while, torturing him psychologically until they fed him to an amoeba. Ed almost got to him in time. Usually R-and-R for a recon agent meant relaxation and fraternization. Ed couldn't shake the guilt and spent most of his time sitting in his room and thinking. He filed for a transfer from recon, and the Elders assigned him riot control. It helped a bit, because most of the time he could take out his aggression on angry mobs. The rules for engagement sat in a gray area on riot control.

The dossier stared back at him. He took a sip of the concoction the doctors had given him. He had requested something to help calm his nerves. Even after the regular debriefing protocol and selective memory wipe, guilt still haunted him. Reluctantly Ed crawled out of bed and picked up the dossier. He sat down at a small table and opened the file. Immediately Ed's mood dropped a notch. When he saw the words *Sub Blackness Cult* at the top of the dossier, he sighed. Ed stood up and walked over to his bed and grabbed his doctor-prescribed pick-me-up.

He took a big sip and then paused. "Ah, fuck it," he said, and drank the rest of the mixture.

Ed's head felt light, and he sat back down in his chair. He picked up a picture in a frame from the corner of the desk. He looked at himself and Ashley standing over their first kill on the surface: a simple drone that had ventured too far for its own good. Ed noticed how short Ashley's hair was at the time, and he noticed that he wasn't bald. With a shaking left hand, he rubbed his head. Long gone were the days when he could grow any more hair. Ed wondered about Ashley. He couldn't get any exact information on the recon agents' assignments now that he had transferred, but his sources mentioned an Observer. Ed grimaced at the thought. Nothing ever happened with that stupid experiment. No successful recoveries and many dead recon agents were the only things he had ever heard about. Rumor had it that the Sub Blackness Cult had gained prominence from recon agents tracking an Observer.

Ed slumped in his chair and looked into the mirror that hung on the wall across from him. He looked like shit. Dark circles surrounded his eyes, and a patchy, unshaven face stared back at him. He couldn't force himself to smile. That part of him had died. He wasn't the only one, either. Many people had stopped smiling or being happy, period. Nobody even bothered faking it anymore either. A general group misery seemed to engulf the base. "And here we have you, Mr. Sub Blackness guy," he mumbled.

Regretfully, Ed turned the page on the dossier and began to read about his assignment. He skipped the case numbers and PC-speak and dived right into the meat of the file. It took Ed more than two hours to read it. He had to stop every so often. The Sub Blackness people had always bothered him. He tossed away most of what the file contained as Elder-speak. If he wanted the answers, the real answers, he needed to meet with his guy.

Ed closed the file and stretched.

A soft computerized female voice, said, "Please note that you have excess water stored up. Failure to use your water will result in forfeiture of your reserve. Three days remaining until reset of water storage."

Hmm, Ed said to himself, *do I need a shower?* He raised his arm and quickly turned up his nose. Ed couldn't remember the last time he had showered or shaved. He looked around the room and saw that bits of half-eaten food and garbage littered the corners of his quarters. "Uh, man, I've let myself go," he muttered, kicking a dirty shirt into a pile of garbage in the corner.

Ed walked away from his desk and entered the bathroom. He turned on the shower and began to wash. Normally he finished quickly, but he had plenty of water in reserve and decided to let the warm water fall around him. He held his head against the wall of the shower and closed his eyes. He stood there until the water expired.

"Water reserves used. Water privileges suspended for one week. Have a nice day."

"Stupid bitch," mumbled Ed. He walked over to the small mirror just outside the shower and began to shave his patchwork beard. His skin burned, and he scooped up the remaining water that had gathered at the bottom of the shower to wash his face. Ed walked out of the bathroom and grabbed his black Hawaiian shirt and jeans. He put on a pair of sandals and headed out the door. "Shit," he mumbled, turning back.

Ed retrieved a piece of cardboard from underneath his mattress and placed it on the small bookshelf across from his bed. With the Elder spy camera hidden, he hit a latch on the back of his night table, and a secret drawer opened. He took an old musty book from the hidden space and placed it under his shirt in the front of his jeans. Ed tossed the cardboard into the pile of garbage in the corner and exited his room.

The walk through the barren alleyways of the common area depressed Ed. Most people huddled together in the gutters, starving. Each week rations became tighter, save those in the Elders' favor. No wonder people bought into the Sub Blackness Cult. Getting food and keeping your family safe went a long way nowadays. Ed could feel it in the street. He watched how people treated the military types. The elders had made a wise choice in moving all military housing away from the common areas.

"Hey, baby," called a woman on the corner, laughing. She twirled around, showing her half-naked body. "One week food rations. Anything you want, honey. I do anything, baby."

Ed paused for a moment and looked at the woman. Her body had amazing curves, but her face showed signs of rot. An STD for the new age. Nasty thing, the Rot, unless you consider your dick falling off pleasant. "Not tonight," said Ed.

"You don't know what you're missing, baby," the woman said, and cackled.

More riffraff of the common wandered about. Ed did feel for the sick children, but he couldn't do much aside from tossing them some extra ration cubes once in a while. The narrow street opened up into a plaza, and Ed walked over to the building with a neon sign that said "Archives." He briefly looked over his shoulder and then rang the buzzer.

"Enter," said a voice through the COMM.

The door open with a buzzing sound, and Ed walked into the Archives. His eyes took a few minutes to adjust to the light. A thick haze of smoke filled the room, emphasized by the numerous neon signs that adorned the walls. A few tables with chairs filled most of the space. One computer per table collected dust. Nowadays those were mostly for show. Most people had given up caring.

"Yanti," said Ed. "Yanti, I don't have time for games."

The lights flickered in the room, and a small buzzing sounded. "I see you have the black shirt on today. Must be serious," said Yanti. He walked into the room abruptly and sat down at a table. A black tank top covered his chest, and ripped jeans and socks the rest of him.

Ed laughed and said, "I see you still have a thing about shoes, Yanti."

"What do you want, Ed?" Yanti asked.

"I need some information."

"What else is new."

"This is different," said Ed. "I need archives from West Coast Elders—a list of known disappearances over the last year, and info on Ashley."

"That's going to cost you," said Yanti as he lit up a smoke.

"Can you get the info?" asked Ed.

"Would you have come here if I couldn't?" retorted Yanti. "Let me see the goods."

"I need to know, Yanti," said Ed sternly. "Can you get the info?"

"Yeah," said Yanti, growing irritated. "This dickhead side of you isn't very flattering, Ed."

"Just checking," said Ed. "This is important."

"I figured so when you mentioned Ashley," said Yanti. "You and her still a thing?"

"We never were, Yanti," said Ed.

"That's not what I heard." Yanti laughed and added, "This won't be cheap."

"Got you covered," said Ed, taking the book from under his shirt and giving it to Yanti.

"Holy shit!" exclaimed Yanti. "Where did you get this? Never mind. Step into my office."

"It has a great ending, too," said Ed. He watched Yanti put out his smoke and walk over to the far wall.

Yanti whistled a strange high-pitched variance and a door opened. Ed stepped through, and Yanti closed the door behind them.

The room's shelves and walls contained enough contraband for the Elders to publicly execute Yanti on the spot—all provided courtesy of Ed. Yanti sat at a large computer and began typing. Code flashed on the screen in a blur. The screen grayed out for a minute, and then green letters appeared.

"What's with the funky colors?" asked Ed.

'It's the West Coast Elder archives. Nothing big. Hey, this is a pretty large file," replied Yanti.

"Give me a few hours with it," said Ed.

"No problem," said Yanti.

"Alone, if you don't mind," Ed added gruffly.

"All right, all right," said Yanti, slowly walking out of the room.

Ed closed the door and took a seat at the computer. *This could take a while*, he thought. Most of the info ended up being Elder-speak. The trio of rogue recon agents, Bear, Bird, and Fox, confirmed Ed's suspicions. Something bothered the Elders enough to keep their mission hidden. The video file, however, bothered Ed the most. He replayed the short video over and over, and the black mist couldn't be clearer. No wonder People flocked to the Sub Blackness Cult. The list of missing persons didn't help much. One thing about the underground was the many ways people can die or go missing. A few notations made by family members reported erratic behavior in a few cases but nothing that could tie into the mythical Sub Blackness.

Ed read over the information pertaining to Ashley. The file didn't hold much info on her mission, just the normal Elder-speak. The name John Brightman appeared a few times, but other than that, not much else. Apparently, some things were out of reach even for Yanti. Something did worry Ed while reading the file. He had worked with Ashley for many years. She never had been able to keep her mouth from rambling over the COMM. According to the scant communication files that Yanti could access, no excess chatter from Ashley had appeared in a few days. He turned away from the screen and looked around the room. Yanti had amassed so much junk from the surface that Ed couldn't help but laugh that the Elders considered a three-inch blue troll doll contraband. Feeling that he had found all the information he could, Ed exited the room with its contraband treasure and said his goodbyes to Yanti.

"Hey, Yanti," said Ed.

"Yeah?" answered Yanti.

"I have a bad feeling about something," said Ed, a hint of concern in his tone.

"You worry too much, Ed," said Yanti with a laugh.

"Maybe," said Ed, "but if I were you, I'd seriously consider getting some red-light camo units and supplies. Get on the next jump ship out of here."

"And go where exactly?" asked Yanti.

"To the surface," said Ed.

"Are you nuts?" asked Yanti. "There's a reason we don't go up there, except you recon loons."

"Ex-recon," said Ed. "Don't say I didn't warn you, Yanti."

Yanti lit a cigarette and turned another page of the book. He waved Ed away and returned to reading. Ed looked back at Yanti and then left the archives. He had another day before the raid on the Sub Blackness Cult. Ed decided to go to the Battered Wheel and drink for a bit. Maybe he could pick up some info on the Sub Blackies if he got lucky. All he knew about them pertained to the leader's aliases.

The Battered Wheel hadn't changed much, thought Ed. He motioned to the bartender for his usual, Freshtatine. Hours passed, and Ed imbibed many glasses of Freshtatine—too many. He began to feel tired, so he tossed the barkeep a ration cube and stumbled into the alleyways. Ed's staggered all over the place. The Freshtatine had done a number on him, and he was beginning to feel it. On a normal day he would have heard his attackers coming, but under the effects of the booze, he didn't stand a chance. A metal bar hit the back of his legs and he fell to the ground. The attackers kicked and punched Ed as he curled up in a ball. After a few minutes of the pummeling, one of the attackers reached into Ed's pocket and took his wallet and rations. As quickly as they had hit him, they disappeared into the common, leaving Ed to wallow in a pool of blood and spit. His vision blurred, and he passed out.

Ed woke to the confines of a cell. He lay on a small bed in the corner. Through the cell's open door he immediately recognized riot control headquarters. Ed slowly propped himself up on the edge of the bed and rubbed his head. He winced at the open wound on top of his bald scalp.

"You aren't supposed to be up yet," said a woman as she entered the cell carrying a black bag. A light green jacket covered a white blouse that hung past the waist of light green trousers full of pockets. Black sneakers quieted her footsteps on the cold floor.

"Lesly," remarked Ed, "figures I'd run into you."

Lesly moved quickly toward Ed and slowly pushed him back on the bed. "Sit," she said, "at least until I get a chance to look you over."

"I've got an assignment in a few hours," said Ed.

"Not until I clear you," said Lesley.

Ed rubbed his eyes and winced. "Can you do something about these lights?" he asked.

"Dim the lights in cell B-Five please," said Lesly.

"Sure thing, babe," said a voice through the COMM.

"So now it's *babe*?" Ed said, chuckling.

Lesly poured disinfectant on Ed's facial lacerations. He jumped as the liquid stung him a little. "Sorry," said Lesly. "I honestly don't see how my personal relations are any of your concern, Edward. I dumped you, remember?"

"Aww, come on. I dumped you," said Ed. "Don't lie about it."

Lesly dressed the rest of Ed's wounds and shined a green light in his eyes. She checked his pulse and heart rate. "Here—take these for the pain."

"So I'm clear?" asked Ed.

"Yes," replied Lesly.

"What do you see in him?" asked Ed.

She replied, "He's everything that you aren't—caring, dependable, and with a job where he doesn't leave for months on end."

"He sounds boring," Ed said, laughing as he quickly grabbed her hand and pulled her close to him. "You don't miss it at all?"

Lesly paused and took a deep breath. She didn't pull away from Ed at first but then slowly backed away. "What am I supposed to say?" she asked. "You disappeared and haven't talked to me in months. I've moved on, Edward. I suggest you do the same."

Ed held her hand a bit longer. "I still have some things over at the house. I'd like to stop by and pick them up."

"Nice try, Ed," said Lesly. "I'll bring them by your hole in the wall later. Now if you'll excuse me, they brought in a burn victim who needs my attention. Take the pills for pain as needed. I wouldn't drink while taking them."

Ed watched her exit the cell. He glanced at the clock on the far wall by the office. He had only a few hours until the mission started. Ed forced himself up and headed into the locker room. He kept quiet as members of his squad exchanged banter and prepared for deployment. Ed took two pills out of the bottle Lesly had given him and swallowed them down. He stripped down to his underwear and slid on a white elastic body suit. Ed walked over to the wall at the end of the row of lockers and stood in a large black circle. Mechanical arms extended from the wall and attached pieces of yellow armor to his body. The final piece, a helmet lowered from above, latched around Ed's head. "Voice communication test, please," a soft computerized female voice said.

"Testing, testing, testing," said Ed, his voice amplified through the helmet to sound unnaturally deep, muffled, and intimidating.

"Threat level of voice satisfactory," said the voice.

Ed moved his arms above his head to adjust to the armor and walked out of the locker room. "Armor up, boys," he said. "We move on the target in twenty minutes."

The riot control moved down the streets of the common in unison, each member adorned in yellow-and-black armor. The shoulders had medium-sized spikes attached, large razors adorned the forearms, and the helmets resembled the shape of a hawk. Black stripes ran down the legs, and the face of the helmet carried a black stripe over the eye area. People on the side of the street scurried away like vermin. Shopkeepers closed their shops, and windows and doors shut and locked. Lately, the riot control squad had been involved in violent interactions with their targets. The street in front of the squad opened up. A large archway stood overhead, and in the distance a group of people had gathered. Large trees decorated the left and right sides of the area. Round flower beds with blue tulips and red roses filled up more of the space. The ground, covered in cobblestone and worn from countless footsteps, held the soft hue of the flowers' colors that reflected from the lighting above. Months ago, when the morale of the common sat at a tolerable level, people used this place to relax and spend an afternoon enjoying the pleasant smell of nature. It was one of the few places underground that provided luxuries of the forgotten surface. Ed looked at the large trees that lined either side of the area acting as a barrier from the shops and huts of the common. The leaves appeared yellowish and green under the pseudo sunlight provided by the soul-stealing lighting of the underground.

"Sniper in position," chattered a voice in Ed's COMM, pulling him away from the tiny bit of serenity the trees and flowers provided.

"Understood," replied Ed. "Moving squad into position."

Ed made a few quick hand movements, and the squad moved forward. Large black shields extended from the left arms of the yellow -and- black armor as the men in the front began to set up a barrier. Other members of the squad moved to the left and right sides. They carried large black rifles. The rifles had blue energy cells near the front. Squad members who didn't carry the rifles armed themselves with rods that crackled energy from the tip.

"Set weapons to stun," said Ed. "Once the sniper has taken his shot and eliminated the target, move in and subdue. I repeat, subdue. I don't want any casualties."

Ed extended a shield from the forearm of his armor suit and moved forward. He pressed the side of his helmet, and his audio unit zeroed in on the speaker addressing the large crowd.

Long white robes extended down the speaker's body to a large pair of black boots. His face appeared thin and was framed by long wavy black hair. His skin was pale and his eyes were dark as the night sky looked at the crowd. "Brothers and sisters, our time is almost here. Our numbers grow stronger every day. You have seen the video of the Black Mist, our savior, that the Elders tried to hide from you. Their lies no longer will enslave us. No more shall they withhold food and water from you. No more shall we wallow in pain and misery as they sit in decadence along with all who serve them. The brothers from the west have succeeded in their task. As I speak, they are spreading his word through the wastes of the west. Our size and lines of communication have both become stronger. I know it's been a long wait, but the time is almost at hand. Soon your loved ones who have gone into the Sub Blackness will meet you. The Black Mist assures me of this. There is but one who stands in our way, my brothers and sisters: the Brightman. Our brethren from the west have set forth to find him. Once he is gone, nothing will stop us from regaining what is ours. This Brightman is responsible for the hell we live in, along with the Elder council." The speaker paused and then said, "Look, my family, the Elders have sent their soldiers to silence me."

The crowd turned around and looked at the riot squad. They produced makeshift weapons from underneath their tattered robes and clothing. Ed motioned to the men in the front lines, and they braced their shields.

"I have a clear shot," said the sniper in Ed's COMM.

"Take him out," ordered Ed.

The sniper in a tall building well behind the riot squad centered his scope on the head of the speaker. The reticle glowed red. The man's finger gently pressed the trigger, and a flash escaped the long rifle. A few feet in front of the speaker, a large blue explosion sent sparks into the air, casting an eerie glow on the crowd.

"Shit, there's an energy shield," said the sniper. "I can't get to the target."

"Didn't see that one coming," said Ed.

"Look, my brothers and sisters, the Elders cannot hurt me. They've come to silence us, as I told you they would. It is time for you to protect

43

what you believe in. Give your lives for the Black Mist. Reap the rewards you seek. Strike now!"

The speaker raised his hands, and the crowd began to run toward the riot squad, weapons swinging wildly in the air. As the followers attacked, the speaker slunk into the shadows and disappeared within the maze created by the streets of the common.

The first wave of the speaker's followers crashed into the wall of shields. Their makeshift knives, axes, clubs, and spears bounced harmlessly away, but the force of their assault sent riot squad members falling backward. A wave of bodies crashed together. A few of the riot squad members fell to the ground, and the followers battered them with their crude weapons. Blood splattered onto the tulips and roses, and the air soon became filled with garbled screams.

Ed met an onrush of followers and used his shield to bash the mob, and his stun rod to down a few more. He spun around, using his shield to create space. A rusty knife smashed against his back, but his armor deflected the weapon. His squad members to the left bashed the crowd with their shields and used the razors on their forearms to cause more followers to stagger. Then Ed heard the shots.

Across the way, blue blasts from the energy rifles cut through bodies, sending blood splattering in all directions. Followers began to drop to the ground, their bodies bearing fatal wounds from the rifle blasts. Blood began to rain down in the area, covering the tree leaves and flowers with its red hue.

"Who's using live rounds?" screamed Ed as he put down another rioter with his stun rod. "I said to subdue—not to kill!"

The followers' cries filled the air, and one by one their screams faded into the common. The sound of the riot controls voices through the authoritative voice modulation and splattering blood replaced their death screams. Ed walked through the fallen corpses and grabbed a rifle out of the hands of one of his squad members. The gun felt hot to the touch, almost overloaded from the energy used.

"Enough," said Ed. "Who started shooting?"

His squad members stood in silence. Ed tossed the rifle aside and walked past his men into the back alleyway. He needed a minute. Thick red blood trickled into a gutter in the alley. Ed shook his head in disgust.

"That's it, *mamacita*, you know what's good for you!" moaned a man. The voice amplifier of the helmet made him sound like a monster. A woman with long dark hair and dark skin screamed in agony. Her dress had been ripped apart by her attacker, exposing her naked body. "I bet you're enjoying this. Oh, yeah!"

"Jones," screamed Ed, "cease and desist now! That's an order!"

"In a minute," Jones grunted. "I'm almost done. That's right, *mamacita*, I'm gonna give you something special!"

Ed reached to his belt and withdrew his sidearm. The woman's screams tore at his mind. He saw her eyes begging for anyone to help. Her arms flailed against the rapist, but she could not do anything to overpower him.

"I said cease and desist now, Jones!" Ed said sternly, pointing the pistol at the man's head.

Jones turned and stared down the gun. "What the fuck, Ed! I'll give you a turn. Just wait a minute."

Without flinching, Ed pulled the trigger. Jones's brains splattered against the alley wall and covered the woman's face and exposed chest. Ed pulled the dead man off her. She began crying. "Go! Get out of here!" yelled Ed.

"My son," she cried. "My son was in the crowd. Where is he?"

"I'll find him," said Ed. "Now get out of here before more men show up. I can't protect you from all of them. Go!"

"My son has a lion tattoo on his left arm," she said. The woman pulled her ripped dress around her and ran away into the common.

Ed put away his pistol and walked back to the carnage. Most of the squad began to clean up. Ed ignored them and walked through the dead bodies.

"Let's go, Ed," said one of his squad members. "The meat wagons are on their way. They'll clean up this mess. We did all we could."

"In a minute," said Ed.

"All right, whatever, man. Hey, you see Jones anywhere?"

"He's around the back alley," said Ed. "One of the rioters shot him. Sorry."

His squad member waved at Ed and left him with the garden of bodies. Ed walked through the dead, checking the left arms as he went.

He checked about a dozen or so bodies until he found the lion tattoo. Ed squatted down and looked at the young man's face. "A teenager," mumbled Ed.

"Help me," cried a voice. "It hurts ..."

Ed turned around and walked over to the mysterious voice.

An older man with his guts hanging out looked up at him. "My back. My back is broken," he gurgled. "Please ..."

Ed paused for a moment, and then a blade extended from just above his hand. Ed raised his arm and plunged the blade into the old man's chest. The man coughed up thick red blood, and life escaped his body. Ed placed his hand over the old man's face and gently closed his eyelids.

Large men in clear hazmat suits shuffled through the carnage. They stuck the dead with large hooks and dragged the bodies to a dozen black vans. One by one they tossed the bodies inside. When one van filled up, the doors closed, and another took its place.

"What the hell happened here?" one of the men asked Ed.

"Just another wonderful day in the common," said Ed.

The man in the hazmat suit grabbed Ed's shoulder and produced a large needle from his belt. "Extend your arm, please," he said.

Ed shrugged off his arm and hesitantly extended his right arm. The man shined a green light across Ed's arm, and a piece of the yellow armor slid back to expose Ed's skin. "This is just a precaution," said the man in the hazmat suit as he pushed the syringe into Ed's skin. "We don't want the Rot transmitted to anyone if any of the dead have it."

The injection stung a bit and left a large welt on Ed's arm. The armor covered his exposed skin, and the man in the hazmat suit returned to dragging dead bodies into the vans for disposal. Ed shook his head to drive the imagery of death away from his mind and headed back for his usual debriefing and report.

THE SPEAKER

The Speaker slunk into the shadows away from the violence facilitated by the riot squad. He knew the mazelike streets of the common like the back of his hand, and cut through various alleyways to gain distance from the bloodshed. The streets of weathered cobblestone stayed dark as night from scattered street lighting that offered few windows for prying eyes. The darkness gave the Speaker the perfect cover for his escape. The sound of riot squad boots occasionally echoed in the distance. Every time the thuds of heavy steps on cobblestone grew closer, the Speaker would turn down another back alley and lose his pursuers.

Upon turning down the last alley, the Speaker stumbled upon a small group of people gathered around a sick man lying in the street.

"Can you please help us? My husband is sick," said an older woman. Her ragged clothes clung to her thin body. A teenage boy and young girl huddled around her feet, their clothes in a similar state.

The Speaker hesitated at first, and then knelt down by the sick man. "How long has he been sick?" he asked.

"A few days," said the older woman. "I don't understand how he can be so ill."

"He's dying," said the Speaker. "He has the Rot."

"Is there anything you can do?" she asked. "The Elders can help. I've seen the soldiers given needles."

"The Elders care not for people like us," said the Speaker. "I can help ease his pain, but I cannot cure him. If you pledge yourself to the Sub Blackness, I will help him. You will be reunited with him when the Black Mist rises."

"I'll do anything," said the woman. "Please help him."

The Speaker placed his hand on the sick man's head and began to mumble words in a language not common to the ear.

The sickly man closed his eyes and asked, "What's happening?"

"Be calm," said the Speaker. "I'm taking you to a place where you will feel pain no longer."

The man said, "No, I don't want to go ..."

Blackness surrounded the Speaker and the man. The family members disappeared from view.

"Stand up," said the Speaker.

The man slowly stood up. He felt better. The poison of the Rot had left his body, and a refreshing feeling washed over his mind. Strength returned to his muscles. "Where am I?" he asked.

"You're in the Sub Blackness," said the Speaker. "I've brought you here to cure your sickness."

"But my family," said the man, "where are they?"

"You will see them in time," said the Speaker. "Now I want to show you something."

The Speaker ushered the man through the blackness. The two walked for what seemed like hours traversing the ever-shifting environment. Red eyes would appear every so often, watching the two men. The sound of machinery rose from the confines of the blackness. Its unseen orchestra filled the area with a deafening mixture of metal screeches, gears, pistons, and drilling. "What is that sound?" asked the man.

"Pay no heed," said the Speaker. "We are almost there."

"Where?" asked the man. "All I see is black."

The Speaker stopped and said, "We are here."

"I don't see anything," said the man.

The Speaker slowly backed away from the man and said, "You will."

"Where did you go?" asked the man, growing uneasy. He stumbled forward through the blackness for a moment longer, but then could not move. His legs froze on the ground. He tried with all his strength but could not will his body to respond. "What's going on?" he asked nervously.

Slithering sounds crept up from behind the man, and two large tentacles blacker than the surroundings wrapped around his arms. The dark forms were of wide girth, and slime from their tough hide dripped

48

over the man's body, burning his bare skin. The tentacles tightened their grip around the man and pulled him backward with ease. The Speaker watched the man disappear into the blackness. Soon the man's screams filled the area. The sound of flesh ripping and bones breaking danced through the Speaker's ears. Blood slowly ran across the ground, its red color growing bright in the darkness. The blood flowed across the floor slowly until it began picking up speed like a river. The Speaker raised his arms toward the blackness as the blood flowed around his legs and up to his knees.

"More," whispered a raspy voice. "Bring more."

"In time, my lord," said the Speaker. "Our plans are almost complete."

"I need more," said the raspy voice, its tone growing darker. "I am still weak. Bring me more. Remember how I found you, Ebene, or have you forgotten suffering from the Rot?"

"No, my liege," said the Speaker as a thin mist flowed around his head and surrounded his body.

"Good," said the raspy voice. "I can return you to that state I found you in if you fail to hold up your end of the bargain. You would succumb to the Rot, an extremely painful and prolonged way to die. I don't believe you truly remember, Ebene. Perhaps I should remind you."

Memories that he did not want to revisit began to fill Ebene's thoughts. The Black Mist forced him to remember. Ebene lay in a dimly lit hospital room that held twenty other beds. In each bed a suffering Rot victim toiled near death, endless waves of pain and discomfort coursing through their bodies. In the various patients, the Rot progressed through its stages at different levels. Some people's arms and legs were amputated in an effort to stop the Rot from spreading. In other cases, tongues, eyes, noses, and mouths infected with boils and green puss marked the last stages of the life cycle of the disease. Ebene blocked out the screams of those in the room. Nurses and doctors wearing clear hazmat suits walked among the forsaken. The nurses tried to offer kind words of hope as they injected pain medication into the dying in an effort to create a false sense of contentment and help ease their torture from the biological nightmare. He looked at his arms and quickly turned his sight to the white ceiling, averting his eyes from the boils and open wounds the Rot had caused. That is when he saw it. A shadowy figure hovered above him. Its form wasn't consistent with anything of this world. The figure lowered until it was just inches above Ebene's ravaged body. Small strings of black mist extended from the ever-changing monstrosity and danced along Ebene's skin, and then gently plunged into his flesh. He winced and slowly began to relax. His body felt different. The pain of the Rot left, and a sense of euphoria cascaded throughout his insides, flowing like lifeblood.

"Feels nice?" asked the figure, its voice low and raspy.

"Yes," said Ebene. "What's going on?"

"I can help you," said the voice. "I will cure you and give you life that none of these other poor souls will have."

"How?" asked Ebene.

"All you need to do is trust me," whispered the voice. "I will need you to help me in exchange."

"Anything," said Ebene. "I'll do anything."

"*Anything* is a very vague term, Ebene," said the voice. "My task is simpler and concise. Will you help me?"

"Yes," said Ebene, "I'll do anything to be rid of this Rot."

"Good," said the voice.

The Speaker remained silent as the memories of his agreement with the mist remained in his thoughts. The blood that flowed around his knees slowly receded. He lowered his arms, and the blackness began to fade away as the mist melted into the Sub Blackness. Hundreds of red eyes watched the Speaker dematerialize and then scurried into the corners of broken thoughts. The back alleyways of the common returned. The Speaker shut the eyes of the sickly man and stood up. "He is in a better place now," he said.

The old woman covered her face with her hand and began sobbing. Her children hugged her waist.

"He won't feel any more pain," said the Speaker. "I gave him a peaceful death. The Rot would have ravaged his body, and he would have suffered."

The old woman wiped her eyes and asked, "What do you want from us?"

The Speaker reached into his pocket and gave the family a week's supply of ration cubes. "Come to the next meeting. All will be explained.

I ask only for your loyalty in these times of darkness. My followers will be rewarded."

The older woman took the rations and placed them into her pocket. "Thank you," she said.

"I must go now," said the Speaker. "My followers will offer you protection and provide you with food. In return you will pledge your loyalty."

The woman nodded and put her arm around her children. "Thank you," she said.

"Return to your home. My followers will come get you when you are called upon," said the Speaker. "You didn't see me today, understand?"

"Yes," replied the woman.

"Very good," said the Speaker. "Now walk in peace."

The older woman watched the Speaker disappear into the shadows of the common's alleyways. She took one last look at her dead husband and ushered her children to walk with her. "What happened to Daddy?" asked the young girl.

"He's in a better place," said the woman, "but we will see him again."

"I'm hungry, Mommy," said the girl.

"Thanks to the nice man, we have food now," said the woman.

"Is that the man who helped Daddy?" asked the girl.

"Yes," replied the woman.

"Did he send him to heaven, Mommy?" asked the girl.

"Yes, he did," said the woman, smiling as she handed her children some of the ration cubes.

The old man's body lay lifeless on the side of the common's cobblestone streets—another faceless victim of the blackness that seeped into the thoughts of the people and throughout the underground. Rats quickly attacked the body, their hungry mouths eagerly picking at the dead man's flesh. Soon they covered his body, their sharp teeth digging into the man's soft, dead skin. The rats moved as a machine over the body, some fighting with others for pieces of the man's flesh. As one rat fell from his corpse, another took its place. A symphony of squeaks and tearing flesh filled the air. With the same quickness and mechanical precision with which the rats had appeared, they departed in unison, having stripped the man's flesh from his bones, and moved back into the shadows of the common. The man's eyes were now gone because of the hungry rats, revealing hollow sockets to stare back into the darkness, and his bones bided their time for the disposal team, waiting for discovery until the organized undertakers made their daily rounds, picking up the dead and heartlessly disposing of the corpses without regard to any previous existence. The disposal team ran like clockwork, a devious but necessary parasite of the daily goings-on in the underground. Lives forgotten as a shared fate suffered regardless of the significance each individual life held. They were processed as a number in a catalog to keep tabs on the population, giving the Elders excuses to cut rations further.

In the Sub Blackness, the old man's mind floated within a black mist, his body now gone, given to the faceless creatures that inhabited the dark domain. The man noticed stray thoughts passing through his mind—thoughts not his own. They began to merge with his consciousness. Soon he began to forget about himself and his family. He began to grow into a greater collective of misplaced musings. Sight slowly returned to the old man, his human form replaced by the ethereal embodiment of two small red eyes. He could move freely within the Sub Blackness, observing everything around him. Other pairs of eyes shared the endless nightmare, and they moved as one through the blackness. The Black Mist left him with the other eyes. They cowered in the corners of the blackness, hiding from their malevolent master, avoiding his cruelty, malice, and hatred whenever they could.

The red eyes began to notice strange things not born of the blackness appearing at random points. Flashes of surreal scenes would break into the void, often surrounded by a subtle white light. The mist would quickly drive away the images, burying them under a series of shackles and locks, but somehow, they would return. So far, the instances focused on the silhouettes of a man and a woman against a backdrop of a destroyed world devoid of laughter. An aura surrounded the man, shining like a beacon in the Sub Blackness. The red eyes could only observe the occurrences. The images birthed a curiosity within the eyes. They possessed no thoughts of their own, but something stirred deep within their ethereal form—possibly a reminder of past happiness or what they used to be. Curiosity created a sense of urgency within the collective existence of the entities, a desire overlooked by the black mist that traveled the areas of the Sub Blackness. Perhaps the persistence of their old selves generated a newfound feeling of hope for the red eyes that the black mist did not foresee—a longing to return to their friends and relatives and look upon the barren and deprived world of the underground again.

Every so often the collective consciousness shared by the eyes screamed in agony. A mixture of their past and present ran together, pushing events from their former lives out of the heavy chains that held them down. The collective mind quickly subdued the images for fear the black mist would punish them. The lack of a physical form did not mean the mist could not harm the misplaced energy their former selves had become. Even in what seemed like death, the black mist could trigger pain and anguish in the collective mind, creating endless suffering within the confines of their prison. So, the red eyes quietly observed and stayed in the corners of the Sub Blackness, perhaps waiting for a random light in the darkness ...

THE BIRD TAKES
FLIGHT

Jessup walked down the hallway leading to his quarters. He decided to turn in for the night. As he walked past one of the rooms, he heard raised voices arguing. One of them belonged to Marybeth, the old woman who had chastised Bird during the meeting. Jessup possessed an intense curiosity that caused him to get into a bit of trouble from time to time. Sure enough, his curiosity won over his better judgment again. He carefully approached the door and knelt down to peer through the tiny keyhole. Marybeth sat at a table. She spoke to someone, but Jessup couldn't make out whom. Her hands were flailing about in agitation.

"That woman is unnatural," she said. "She came from the west out of nowhere. Has a baby and her hair color changes overnight. I think we should take the baby. Have tests done on it. The scientists are hiding something from us."

"If Devin finds out that we took her baby, he'll throw us into the wild," said a man.

Jessup couldn't discern who the man was. He could see only Marybeth. "We need to do this quickly. Not give Devin enough time to react. If you're wrong and nothing is unusual with the child, Devin will not be happy."

"There's something not right with that child," said Marybeth. "I'm sure of it."

"I'll notify the others, and we'll move on this tomorrow night," said the man.

"Agreed," said Marybeth.

Jessup stepped back from the keyhole in horror. He had to warn Bird. Jessup turned and quickly walked down the hall toward Bird's room. Two large men in black fatigues stood guard at Bird's door. Jessup surmised they probably wouldn't let him in, so he made a tiny plan. He entered the supply room a few doors down from Bird's quarters and grabbed some towels and filled a bowl with water. He placed them on a tray and headed back toward Bird's room.

"I've brought supplies for the baby," said Jessup to the large men in front of Bird's door. "Changing supplies."

"No one is permitted to see Miss Bird except doctors or the midwife," said one of the men.

"If I don't get these changing supplies to Bird, things are going to begin to stink," said Jessup. "It's fine if you guys want to smell fresh baby poop all night. I can just put these supplies back ..."

One of the men shifted his stance. "Fine, but make it quick. Miss Bird needs rest."

"Gotcha," said Jessup. "I'll be quick."

The two men moved aside, and Jessup slowly opened the door and closed it behind him. He placed the tray on the floor and walked over to Bird, who lay asleep on her bed. Jessup looked over her sleeping body. Bird's curves enticed Jessup and excited him. He looked at her soft, peaceful face lost in sleep. Jessup sat gently on the edge of the bed and touched Bird's shoulder. "Bird," said Jessup. "Bird, wake up, please. It's Jessup."

Bird shifted for a moment, and then opened her blue eyes. "Jessup, what are you doing here?"

"Bird," said Jessup, his voice filled with concern, "there's something wrong. Trouble."

"Trouble?" said Bird. "What are you talking about?"

"I overheard Marybeth and someone saying they are going to take your child," said Jessup.

Bird propped herself up on her elbows and looked at him. "What?"

"They plan to do it tomorrow night," said Jessup.

"Jessup," said Bird, "this is crazy. Are you sure about this?"

Jessup nodded. "Definitely. I heard it with my own ears."

Bird sat up now, her back against the wall. "She will not touch my child," said Bird. "Over my dead body."

"We can let Devin know," said Jessup. "He can stop her."

"I'm leaving, Jessup," said Bird.

Shocked, Jessup said, "Leaving? But why?"

"It's not safe here for me anymore," said Bird.

"Devin can handle Marybeth and her cronies," said Jessup. "Just let me talk to Devin."

"I'm not worried about Marybeth," said Bird. "It's something else, something worse."

"I'll help you, Bird," said Jessup. "We can leave together."

Bird put her hand on Jessup's shoulder and looked at him with her soft blue eyes. "That's sweet, Jessup, but I can take care of myself."

"You have a baby to watch over, Bird," said Jessup. "You can't do this alone. Tell me what's going on."

Bird lowered her head and stayed silent for a few minutes. Leaf shifted in his crib and let out a few low cries. Bird walked over to him and took Leaf in her arms. He giggled and closed his eyes, his tiny body nestled in his mother's arms. Jessup did make sense, Bird thought. Taking care of Leaf and keeping herself alive could be easier with someone helping her. "I received transmissions in my helmet, Jessup."

"Other people," said Jessup. "That's good. Maybe they can help us."

"Not these people," said Bird. "My helmet couldn't decrypt two of the transmissions, but it identified the language used as Robot."

"You mean the Robots that devour our brains and wear our skin? Those kind of Robots?" asked Jessup.

"Yes," said Bird, "those kind of Robots."

"How?" asked Jessup.

"I don't know, but some people in this settlement are not human," said Bird. "Where there are Robots, creatures are sure to follow."

"This isn't good," said Jessup. "Do you think Marybeth is one of them?"

"It could be anyone," said Bird, "even you."

"I'm not a Robot," said Jessup. "Crap, Bird, you should know that."

Bird looked at Jessup again. His eyes showed a bit of pain from her accusation. He truly did care about her. "Sorry, I didn't mean it," she said.

"It's all right," said Jessup. "What did you have in mind? If we just leave, Devin may get suspicious and detain us. This settlement feels more and more like a prison every day."

"We can leave tonight in secret," said Bird, "but we'll need supplies to take with us. The third transmission my helmet decrypted after searching through its database is an old frequency used by the military. As of now, it's too far away to pinpoint, but the general direction is east."

"I can gather supplies," said Jessup.

Bird nodded and said, "Meet me at the greenhouse in an hour. The sooner we leave here, the better."

"Great," said Jessup. "I'll see you then."

"Be careful," said Bird.

"Of course," replied Jessup. Excited, he stood up and waved his goodbyes, and then exited the room.

Bird placed Leaf back in his crib and walked over to the box that contained her gear. She opened the lid and looked at her jumpsuit. "I never thought I'd have to use you again."

Bird took off her loose-fitting white gown and slipped into her jumpsuit. The material still fit the curves of her body snugly. She pulled her hair into a ponytail and slipped on her helmet. Bird picked up the katana from the box and sheathed it over her back. She grabbed a makeshift pouch from the foot of her bed and fastened it to the front of her jumpsuit. She attached the old radio to her left shoulder. Then she covered Leaf in his scarlet wrap and gently placed him in the pouch on her chest. The device held him securely and left Bird's arms and hands free. With Leaf safe against her chest and all her gear at the ready, Bird walked over to the lone window in her room and pushed it open. She paused and then went back to the box and picked up a black notebook, her journal. She returned to the window and deftly stepped through the opening, nimbly crawling up an escape ladder on the side of the building. The sky was devoid of the usual red and purple clouds, which allowed stars to cast their shine for the naked eye to discern. A bright moon offered enough light to navigate the dark of night.

Jessup made his way through the settlement to the supply room. He wasn't surprised to find that Devin kept the doors locked. Jessup sighed slightly and then reached into his pocket and pulled out a small pouch. He produced a set of thieves' tools: a thin, flexible metal wire and a thicker metal piece with an L-shaped head. Jessup inserted the tools into the lock and twisted the metal around. He listened to the tiny and subtle sound of tumblers falling into place one by one. After a few more twists and prods, the lock popped open and Jessup opened the door. Moonlight dimly lit the room from glass windows in the ceiling. Jessup searched around and found a black backpack. He grabbed two flashlights, a few trays of rations and water, medical supplies, blankets, a utility knife, changing supplies for Leaf, and a small torch to produce flame. *Can't pass this up*, thought Jessup as he put a large bottle of red wine into the backpack. The supplies seemed archaic amidst a world steeped in technology. Jessup moved to the back of the room and found a lockbox. He used his thieves' tools again to open the box. Inside sat a phase pistol, holster, and extra energy cell. Jessup took the weapon and ammo from the box and attached the holster to his hip. He secured the pistol in the holster and strapped on the backpack full of supplies.

"Did you leave the door open?" asked a man's voice.

"No," said another man.

"Let's check it out."

Jessup heard the men's voices cut through the silence. He moved quickly and hid behind one of the racks in the middle of the room. Shelves lined the walls of the storage area, and a few racks created aisles within the middle of the room. The lights turned on as the men entered the room.

Jessup made himself small behind the end of a rack. He peered down the aisle and watched the men sift through the supplies. As the men moved closer to Jessup, he slowly and quietly slunk away in the opposite direction. Jessup moved to the main entrance, and while the men were rounding the aisles, he crept out the door and moved down the hall. That is when Jessup heard the explosion. He couldn't tell where it had originated. Red lights in the hallways turned on, and the fire alarm sounded.

"Warning, exterior breach," boomed a computerized voice. "Lockdown procedures commencing. Please return to your quarters."

Jessup heard people screaming and shouting. Strange guttural roars drowned out the screams. He ran down the hall and turned a corner.

A geyser of blood shot upward. A large creature with powerful, thick legs held someone in its grasp. A round head sat atop the body, and a tube extended from the creature's maw. The tube engulfed the person's head. Blood quickly drained from the person's body through the tube. Jessup ran toward the far door in front of the two, quickly entered the room, and then shut the door and pushed a bookshelf in front of it. He could hear the sound of bones breaking and then a loud shriek from the creature. Heavy fists pounded on the door, each hit weakening the structure. Jessup looked around and saw a window at the far end of the room. He looked out the window. "Oh shit," he said. "This might hurt!"

Jessup jumped through the window, using his arms to shield his eyes from the broken glass. He landed in a heap and grabbed his leg. Men in black fatigues ran through the courtyard with rifles. Gunfire erupted all around Jessup. He regained his wits and headed toward the greenhouse. Bodies lay strewn about on the ground along with dead creatures, their remains a mass of tentacles, slime, and deformities. Through the smoke that now billowed into the area, Jessup could discern the greenhouse up ahead. He continued on, dodging roaming creatures as he could, using the scant shadows provided by the night as cover. Jessup pulled his green shirt over his mouth and nose to help with the thick smoke. Flashing red lights lit up the area, and he opened the greenhouse door. Tall sunflowers made up the majority of the middle of the greenhouse. Various medicinal herbs grew in small trays along the sides. Red, blue, purple, yellow, and orange flowers cast a calming color into the area reflected from the moonlight. Jessup could see creatures through the glass. They hunted in the darkness for their prey. The creatures moved quickly, their powerful legs propelling them from one victim to the next.

The sound of breaking glass from above cut into the serenity of the greenhouse. A larger creature on four legs fell through the glass and landed amongst the tall sunflowers. Loud grunts filled the greenhouse. The sunflowers slowly fell one by one in Jessup's direction as the creature ripped them from the earth with its large maw filled with razor-sharp teeth. Two large arms with claw hands extended from the creature's back and tossed sunflower plants aside. Jessup backed up slowly. He grabbed the phase pistol from its holster and took aim at the falling plants. Finally, the creature uprooted the last few sunflower plants and Jessup could see its cold black eyes. His arm began to shake as the creature turned its attention to the prey that quivered in front of it.

Glass on the far wall shattered, and a light blue flash cut across Jessup's vision. Moonlight reflected the silver of a katana as it cut through the air. The katana's slash separated one of the creature's large arms from its body. Bird fell to one knee in front of the creature, holding her blade at the ready. Green blood spurted out from the wound, and the creature staggered back for a moment. Then it rose onto its back legs and roared. Flesh on the creature's face flared out, and a large black tongue whipped about within its maw. Bird stood up and used the katana to slash quickly across the creature's midsection. Green blood sprayed into the air, splattering on the glass of the greenhouse. The creature winced and collapsed to the ground, its body cut into two pieces, spilling a large pile of guts onto the ground.

"Bird!" shouted Jessup. "Bird, you made it!"

"Let's go!" shouted Bird.

Jessup stood in awe of Bird. Her movements were quick and elegant but powerful for such a slight build. He had never seen her in her recon gear. The light blue suit sparkled in the moonlight. Her helmet, in the shape of a blue jay, broke through the jarring scene of death.

"Now, Jessup!" shouted Bird.

Jessup shook his head. "Right! Where are we going? The whole settlement is under attack!"

"Follow me. We're going to the watchtower!"

"But we'll be cornered up there."

"Trust me," said Bird. "Did you get the supplies?"

Jessup pointed to his backpack. "Yes, I picked up what I could."

"Good. Now let's move!" shouted Bird.

Jessup followed behind Bird. He had a hard time keeping pace as she moved with precise and deft motions. Jessup noticed Bird had fasted Leaf to her chest, and the child barely made a sound even in a world surrounded by violence and death. The three of them quickly left the greenhouse, its serene beauty now marred by bloodshed. The few sunflowers that still remained glowed in the moonlight. Their bright yellow petals swayed in the air and shined through the death that permeated the settlement.

The area Bird and Jessup navigated held little cover. Thick smoke from the destruction of the settlement hid their movements and allowed them to gain access to the halls of the dam once again. Bird's helmet emitted a bluish light that scanned the dark hallways. She held her katana at the ready and slowly moved forward. Ahead of them, debris from an explosion blocked the hallway. An open door to the left swayed back and forth in front of the debris. "Through here, Jessup," she said, motioning to the door.

"It's her!" shouted Marybeth peering through an opening in the debris. "Get her!"

Marybeth and a group of people watched as Bird and Jessup entered the room. Debris blocked their progress. "She's getting away!"

"The way is blocked," said a man. "We can't get through."

"We'll have to double back," shouted Marybeth. "She brought these creatures to us!"

Jessup followed Bird into the room and shut the door behind them. Journals and large piles of paperwork littered the floor and shelves. At a large desk a man lay hunched over, a gunshot wound to his head and a pistol in his right hand. The computer in front of him played a message over and over. Jessup nudged the man, and he fell out of the chair onto the floor. "It's Ben," said Jessup. "Devin's chief scientist."

"Look at this," said Bird as she pointed to the computer.

Jessup glanced at the video playing and moved the mouse over to a large icon and clicked on it. The video stopped its loop and started from the beginning. The scientist's image spoke back to Bird and Jessup from the recorded video. "This is chief science officer Benjamin Mitt. Not that my words now will change anything, but I just wanted them on the record. Something isn't right with Devin. During the time we've been at this settlement, he had me contaminate the water supply. I've been using a drug synthesized from dead creatures' cells that causes sterility in the men of the settlement. The effects aren't permanent. The contaminant will leave the body over time. Devin used the excuse that he didn't want the population to outgrow our food supply. At first, I believed him, but then some things didn't add up.

"I can't exactly pinpoint the time Devin changed. I collected a sample of Devin's DNA without him knowing it. The results startled me. Devin isn't human. He isn't a creature, but he's definitely not human. I should have brought this to my colleagues' attentions, but Devin threatened me. Maybe if I had ignored him, none of this would have happened. I sit here as our settlement is under attack and my friends and neighbors are dying in front of my eyes.

"This place is not safe. Anyone who finds this place should leave. The food supply has enough contaminant to cause sterility for another few months. What have I done? There is more. Pressed by Devin, I engineered a virus from a substance found on Bird's jumpsuit. Devin explained the necessity of the situation. Innocent people died because of me. I can't live with this guilt. Forgive me."

The last recorded image showed Ben putting a pistol to the side of his head.

Jessup cut the video and said, "Devin, not human?"

"He's the robot," said Bird. "He brought the creatures here. We've got to get out of here, Jessup. Now!"

Bird smashed the window in the room with her katana and peered up the side of the building. "We can use the ladders and roofs to get to the watchtower."

"I hate heights," said Jessup.

"Just don't look down," said Bird as she exited through a window and climbed up a ladder.

Jessup took a deep breath and crawled through the window. He grabbed the ladder and felt his legs hang free in the air. Regaining his composure, he placed his feet on the rungs and slowly climbed. Bird stood at the top of the roof, looking around the area, until Jessup's head finally appeared. She reached out and pulled Jessup up. "Thanks," said Jessup.

"Only a few more to go," said Bird.

"Great," said Jessup, following Bird up the next series of ladders.

Bird and Jessup arrived at the top of the watchtower, where a trio of men in black fatigues operated a large Gatling gun that shot blue pulses of energy. They focused on winged creatures that swooped and dived over the settlement. Each creature that the energy hit exploded in blood and guts falling into the reservoir. A large winged red creature with an enormous bulbous sack for a belly hovered in the distance. Smaller creatures birthed from the sack assaulted the settlement. "Focus on the big one," said a man in fatigues. Bird remembered him because of his beard. He had brought her the box that contained her equipment.

The other two men moved the large base of the Gatling gun and took aim at the creature birthing the smaller ones. "Put everything you've got on that fucker," said the man with the beard. "Make its blood rain down."

The blue energy from the Gatling gun assaulted the massive creature. Red blood began to pour into the water of the reservoir. More and more of the red blood mixed with the water, its color overtaking the dark black of the reservoir. The energy assault on the creature didn't relent until the birther exploded and fell into the reservoir with an ear-piercing shriek. Its wings flapped in defiance a few times, fighting against the weight of the red water, until it sank into the depths.

The door behind the men crashed open and Devin burst through, holding a rifle. His eyes glowed blue, and his hair burned in the moonlight. He spoke a language not known to the human ear. Devin opened fire on the men at the Gatling gun. He struck two in the chest, and they slumped against the sandbags around the base of the gun, blood splattering against the cold floor of the watchtower. Devin took aim at the man with the beard. Bird quickly stepped in front of him and deflected the shots from Devin's rifle with her katana. The bullets reflected and struck the rifle, breaking it into pieces.

"Get out of here!" shouted the man with the beard. He grabbed a large black satchel from his belt and quickly set the timer to twenty seconds. "Now go!"

Bird watched as the man grabbed Devin with both arms. The two began to struggle, and toppled into the reservoir. "Grab my shoulder, Jessup," said Bird, "and don't let go!"

Jessup hugged Bird from behind, and then moved his hands on her shoulders as instructed. Bird spread her arms outward, and a light blue webbing extended from her hips to her underarms. She looked at Leaf once and then shouted, "Hold on!"

Jessup took a deep breath as Bird jumped from the top of the watchtower. The radio on her shoulder began to sound out adrenaline-pumping guitar riffs. *That's new*, thought Bird. In the distant night sky a bright white lightning bolt sparked, lighting up the area. Bird's body descended quickly, and then air began to catch the webbing that sprouted from her jumpsuit. Jessup and Bird rose into the sky and careened through the rock valley of the river, driven by the sounds of the radio that drowned out the orchestra of screams rising from the inhabitants of the dam.

"I know this song," said Jessup. "Good old Jimmy!"

Deep within the blood-red reservoir, Devin's eyes shined their blue light. Then the night lit up in a bright flash as an explosion escaped the bowels of the reservoir. The shock waves from the detonation cracked the walls of the dam. Water began seeping through slowly and then faster as more concrete broke away, its integrity destroyed by the blast. Jessup turned his head to look back at the explosion and saw the dam burst. The blood-red water of the reservoir flowed into the river. Bird and Jessup soared above the violence. Bird adjusted to the extra weight of Jessup, slipped a bit, and then quickly regained the air current and stabilized their decent. The dam disappeared in the night, left only to memories. Bird and Jessup soared through the night sky for miles, backlit by the soft glow of the moon, and then began to descend. The ground rushed toward them at a quick pace.

"You are going to need to jump now, Jessup," said Bird.

"J-j-jump?" shouted Jessup.

"Yes," said Bird, "or we're both going to die. I can't land safely with the extra weight."

Jessup closed his eyes and let go of Bird. He fell quickly, crashed into the ground, and rolled for several yards. Bird pulled back her arms and slid across the red dust-covered ground, traveling a fair distance before finally stopping. The harmonic sounds of the radio faded away, and Leaf giggled, safely nestled in his carrier. Jessup moaned a few yards away.

Bird walked over to him and knelt down by his head. "Are you all right?" she asked.

Jessup shook his head and swept the red dust off of his clothes. "I think so. Holy shit, Bird, that was crazy. Tell me we didn't just fly!"

Bird laughed a bit. "Not exactly flying—more like gliding."

Jessup stood up and shifted his backpack to a more comfortable spot. "Where are we?"

"Far enough from the dam, for now," said Bird. "The radio transmission my helmet picked up is somewhere due east. I can't pinpoint it yet, but my sensors say it's close."

"East it is," said Jessup.

Back at the dam, the last remaining creatures began to disappear as quickly as they had come. The survivors, crying and screaming in pain, wandered through the dead. Frightened and unsure, they gathered together near the greenhouse.

Marybeth stood atop a high building and looked down at the survivors. Her short black hair, wet from the blood of the dead, clung to her face. She pulled back her hair and wiped away the blood, mixing it into her hair. "Friends," she said, "it was the one from the west. The Bird brought this upon us. It was her and her baby. We cannot let this go unpunished."

The mass of people looked up at Marybeth, desperate for answers and guidance. "Where is Devin?" asked someone in the crowd.

"Killed by Bird," said Marybeth. "Killed by the one he took in."

"Everything happened so fast," said another face in the crowd. "How can you be certain it was her? Maybe she's dead."

"I saw her," said Marybeth, an unnatural rage projecting from her dark brown eyes. "I saw her fly away to the east. We will rebuild, my friends, and grow stronger. We will remember this night and those who brought these creatures to us. The Bird cannot get away with what she has done. She must pay, and her abomination child must be destroyed."

The crowd remained silent, their hopes destroyed as their loved ones' bodies decorated the once prosperous settlement. Marybeth continued to speak, and her words began to resonate with the crowd. Nods of approval spread across the sea of faces.

Clouds rolled into view and blotted out the faint light from the moon. A heavy rain began to fall, washing away the bloodshed and violence from the events of the attack. Marybeth continued to send her demonizing words toward the eager ears of the crowd. In the greenhouse the rain began to trickle onto the sunflowers. Under the weight of the rain they drooped slightly. Water rolled off the yellow petals and fell onto the ground. The flowers gave the illusion of eyes soaked by tears after just witnessing a tragic, incomprehensible act. The rain continued to fall upon the devastation and began to spread farther away from the remains of the dam, covering the barren landscape with its sullen embrace. The blood-red water from the reservoir flowed freely into the rocky landscape fed by the heavy unrelenting rain.

SCRIBBLINGS
WITH CHALK

The last bit of the dark sky faded away as John Brightman kept his firm grip on Ashley. He hadn't slept through the uneventful night. At one point, nightmarish flying creatures shrieked above them but paid them no heed. They moved with speed and ferocity toward the west. A gentle rain began to fall, and Ashley awoke. She turned in Brightman's arms to face him.

"You're growing a beard," she said.

"Oh yeah," said Brightman. "Not much to shave with, honestly. Just easier to grow a beard, I guess."

"I like it," said Ashley as she forced herself up from the comforting sleep. "Where are we?"

"I'm not sure," said Brightman. "After the robots destroyed the ship, you passed out. I carried you as far away as possible."

Using her goggles, Ashley scanned the area. "There's no movement for now. That's a good thing. I don't know what to do now, though. My COMM unit is broken and my ship destroyed. Maybe we can get to an old jump point and wait, but I don't know."

"We can head north," said Brightman. "My dreams suggested we head north."

"Dreams—that may be all we have," said Ashley, laughing. "Before we do anything, I want to take inventory of the rations we have left."

Brightman sat cross-legged and watched Ashley rummage through her duffel bag.

"How did you figure out how to operate the camouflage device?" asked Ashley.

"I'm not sure. Something flashed in my head like in my dream, and I just understood it," said Brightman.

Ashley looked at the device carefully. "You didn't break it. Did you sleep, Brightman?"

"No, someone had to keep watch," he said.

"Well," said Ashley, "we have a week of rations left. Maybe a week and a half if we skip meals here and there. I hope your dreams are right, Brightman."

Brightman rose to his feet and grabbed the duffel bag.

Ashley stopped him and tossed it over her shoulder. "I've got it, Brightman," she said. "Now let's get moving. I want to find someplace to wait out this rain."

Brightman looked up at the red and purple clouds that blocked out the sun. Raindrops fell upon his face and cascaded down his cheeks. Ashley began to walk forward to the north. Brightman wiped the rain from his face and slowly followed after her. His steps labored in the morning rain that grew heavy. In no time the ground became slippery under his feet.

"What exactly did you see in your dreams?" asked Ashley, breaking the constant gentle sound of rain falling.

Brightman paused and then said, "I'm not exactly sure. Mainly everything is black when I dream. Voices told me to go north."

"Great—we're heading into the forgotten zone blind," mumbled Ashley.

"Forgotten zone?" asked Brightman.

"It's an area we recon agents don't venture into unless we have to," said Ashley.

"That doesn't sound good," said Brightman.

"It's not," said Ashley. "There are rock formations over to the right. It shouldn't take more than two or three hours' travel time to reach them. Maybe we can get out of this rain."

Brightman's clothes felt wet to the touch, and the air around him grew cold. The rain continued to fall upon the two as they slowly traveled north not knowing who or what they would find. Every so often Brightman would peer into the hazy distance. He thought he saw the form of a large grizzly bear appear and then quickly dip into the horizon. Brightman and Ashley remained silent for the duration of the walk. He thought of the night before and remembered her heartbeat, a gentle sound in the night that had comforted him. The grizzly bear quickly appeared again and then moved toward the right.

"Up there—do you see that?" asked Brightman, pointing into the haze.

"What are you talking about?" asked Ashley.

"The bear," said Brightman. "You don't see that bear?"

Ashley scanned the area with her goggles. "There's a rock formation over there, but I'm not picking up any life forms on my scan."

"Just humor me," said Brightman. "Let's check it out. I feel like we're being led by something."

"There's nothing out there, Brightman," said Ashley.

Brightman picked up the pace and tracked the image of the grizzly bear that haunted his vision. "This way," he said.

The terrain grew steeper, and the constant rain made the ground cumbersome for their footsteps. Ashley and John had to support each other's weight and balance one another to get up the incline. The rain began to obscure their vision as it fell at a faster pace. Water mixed with the red dust that covered the ground and ran red down the incline. Brightman slipped once and sank his hands into the now soft mud to keep himself from sliding down the hill. He propped himself up and joined Ashley at the top of the incline. On their right, an entrance to a cave cast an invitation to escape from the cold rain. In the distance, creatures shrieked loudly, ever searching for their next meal.

Ashley cracked a black stick and handed it to Brightman. The stick glowed a bright blue and offered illumination to the dark mouth of the cave. Brightman noticed Ashley held her flame unit at the ready and fired a few streaks of orange fire into the cave.

"Let's go," said Ashley. "We can at least get out of the rain for a while."

Brightman held his light high, and the two entered the cave. They ventured forth ten or twenty yards into the depths before the narrow space opened into a larger room. A small pool of water sat in the middle, created by runoff from the heavy rain. Another corridor appeared on the far side of the room. Ashley directed Brightman to follow.

"Wait," said Brightman, "look at this."

John held the blue light in his hand and motioned to Ashley to look at the walls on the left of the open cavern, which were adorned with childlike pictures and scribblings. On a small ledge under the drawings, an open box of chalk appeared out of place within the dull trappings of the cave. The chalk glowed slightly within the darkness in contrast to the weathered rock of the underground passage.

"What's that?" asked Ashley.

"They look like drawings," said Brightman.

The light shined, allowing the pictures to resonate within the dark cave with a distinctness. The lower picture showed a bear in a cage. Brightman followed the pictures up the wall of the cave. A bird flew above the bear, and a fox walked underneath them both. Near the apex of the drawing the three animals sat together, and the large bear pointed toward a building. Brightman followed the pictures along the side of the cavern to the opening of another area that he had not seen earlier.

"I saw these animals in my dreams," said Brightman.

"The drawings look fairly new," said Ashley. "Who could've drawn them?"

Brightman picked up a piece of chalk from the box and began writing on the wall of the cavern. "We saw your message," wrote Brightman in white lettering.

"What are you doing?" asked Ashley.

"Sending a response," said Brightman.

"A response to whom?" asked Ashley.

"Didn't you say something about a lost recon team?" asked Brightman.

"They were located thousands of miles to the west, John," said Ashley.

"I think I've dreamed them," said Brightman.

"That's impossible, Brightman," said Ashley. "The underground lost contact with them."

"Look at this," said Brightman as he shined the light on another image farther down the side passage. A stick figure drawn in green chalk had a large white aura around it. Thoughts of the morning in his bathroom flashed into Brightman's head. Vague images of a bright white light came back to him.

"This passage extends farther," said Ashley.

"Let's check it out," said Brightman.

"Sure, why not," Ashley said, chuckling. "Might as well follow the scribblings in chalk. Voices in dreams and mysterious doodles ..."

"Do you have any better ideas?" asked Brightman.

Ashley didn't respond, and the two made their way deeper into the cavern. The corridor extended for another thirty to forty yards and then opened into another larger room. In the center of the room sat a pile of old toys and books.

Brightman walked over to the pile and sat down. "What's this?" he asked.

Ashley knelt down and picked up an old child's toy. "Toys," she said.

"I know what toys are. How did they get here?" asked Brightman, falling slightly to one side as he spoke.

"You need to get some sleep," said Ashley. The sound of rain reverberated through the cavern, creating a somber mood. "Let's wait out the rain a little longer."

Brightman nodded and put the light stick on the ground. He stretched out and closed his eyes. Before falling into sleep, he watched Ashley sift through the pile of toys. "See something you like?" he asked.

"You don't see toys that often in the underground," said Ashley as she picked up a tiny stick figure made out of white and green yarn.

"It must be tough to live there," said Brightman, attentively watching Ashley sift through the pile.

Ashley placed the yarn figure in the chest pocket of her jumpsuit and said, "Get some sleep."

Brightman didn't want to sleep, but his body began to override his desires. He fell into a peaceful sleep. Fears of the Sub Blackness crept into his thoughts but were washed away by a strange contentment he felt within the damp cavern.

John awoke to a loud crash.

Ashley walked into the area with a concerned look on her face and said, "The cavern entrance collapsed. We can't get out."

Brightman wiped the remnants of sleep from his eyes. He hadn't dreamed, he thought. "How long was I asleep?"

"A few hours," said Ashley. "The rain has stopped."

Ashley gave Brightman a small bit of rations and a water pill. The cavern air gripped their bodies in its cold and clammy embrace.

"I hope this cavern up ahead leads somewhere," said Ashley.

"It will," said Brightman.

"Well, let's go."

Brightman followed Ashley down the corridor. She gave him another light stick. The blue light cut through the darkness and shined for their eyes to navigate the rough terrain of the cavern. Soon the light around them grew brighter and the ground under their feet sprouted scattered green grass. As Brightman and Ashley followed the cavern, sunlight broke across their vision.

Brightman asked," Is that … ? Is that … ?"

"Yes," said Ashley, "it's an exit."

Brightman tossed the light stick aside and walked toward the sunshine. A large opening appeared, allowing a return to the world. Sunlight filled the sky, and the rain became a memory. In front of Brightman a walkway held his vision and on the right side of the path more scattered grass grew. The path gave way to an opening through the rocks. To the left a large pit filled with human skeletons and bones reminded Brightman of the violence the world offered. The skeletons, which numbered in the hundreds, lay heaped upon one another. Occasionally a few randomly stood away from the pile. Brightman noticed two skeletons embracing, offering a last act of love to the heartless world around them. Their actions seemed frozen in time amidst the eerie sense of death that filled the area. The pit's circumference made Brightman take a step back. He had never seen such a large craterlike area. He turned his eyes to the narrow walkway.

"That way," said Brightman. "I think we should go that way."

"Hold on," said Ashley, putting her arm out to stop Brightman.

"What is it?" asked Brightman.

"This area," said Ashley. "I've heard about places like this but have never seen one. During the initial phases of the war, chemical weapons were used against the creatures."

"These skeletons aren't creatures," said Brightman. "They're people."

"The powers in charge didn't care about human casualties if they thought the targets were big enough," said Ashley.

Brightman looked across the area of death and felt sullen. He wondered what had gone through the minds of the innocent victims whose past played out, exposed before his eyes. Across the large pit sat a toppled building. It barely stood more than five feet high now. Red vines that extended from the pit ran into the debris of the building. They wrapped around rock and broken pieces of concrete. Tiny bulbs sprouted off the sides of the vines.

"Tragic," said Brightman.

"We have bigger things to worry about right now," said Ashley, "and I do mean big."

"What do you mean?" asked Brightman.

"Marrow Munchers," said Ashley.

"Marrow Munchers?"

"They're big creatures that nest in areas where large numbers of people died," explained Ashley. "See those things that look like vines over there?"

Brightman nodded. "Yeah."

"Those aren't vines, Brightman," muttered Ashley. "They're parts of a Marrow Muncher."

"Should we go back?" asked Brightman.

"Go back to where?" retorted Ashley. "We'll go up that walkway, carefully."

"Maybe this Marrow Muncher thing is dead," said Brightman.

"Not likely," replied Ashley.

Brightman shuddered and took a deep breath. "What actually does a Marrow Muncher do to people?"

"It sucks the bones from your body," said Ashley. "We should be okay if we don't let it know we're here."

Ashley went forward, staying close to the rock side of the walkway. The ground remained wet from the heavy rain. Brightman followed, staying away from the open ledge near the side of the walkway. One misstep would send him careening into the large pit of bones. Brightman's nervousness spiked as the two inched up the walkway.

Every step induced fear in Brightman. He began to lose focus, and his next step dislodged a large rock and sent it rolling down the path. The rock bounced off the side of the wall and rolled into the pit.

"Oh shit," whispered Brightman.

"Don't move," Ashley said softly.

The rock bounced off of broken skeletons like a pinball. Something moved within the pit. Skeletal bodies churned like ocean waves, and the back of something large poked through the pile of bones. Large, sharp finlike attachments reflected in the sunlight. They appeared bluish green. The vine like growths near the destroyed building disappeared into the pit. The skeletons rolled again as the monstrosity in the pit shifted its weight. The vine like appendages ran up the side of the pit and paused in the air. The bulbs that extended from their sides opened to reveal circular mouths with blunt teeth lining the circumference.

"Run, John," shouted Ashley. "Run!"

Brightman looked behind him and watched the vines slithering toward him. Ashley stepped in front of him and covered the area with a stream of orange flames. The ground caught fire and a flame wall burned. The vines retreated from the flames back into the pit. Brightman felt the ground begin to shake as the large creature within the pit rose from the recesses of the skeletal remains it called home. The creature's skin cast a black sheen in the sunlight. The form, that of a snakelike creature, reached into the sky. Vine like feelers extended from the thick skin and searched the surrounding areas. A large head extended from the end of the snakelike creature. Two black horns protruded from its head. Thin yellow eyes surveyed the area, searching for those who disturbed its slumber. The creature roared in anger, and the ground shook from its rage.

Brightman couldn't move as terror coursed through his body. The creature before him stood taller than a five-story building.

Ashley ran past Brightman and grabbed him by the shoulder, shouting, "Run!"

The paralysis faded, and Brightman ran after Ashley. More vines shot through the air and blocked the walkway. Ashley unloaded a stream of flames into the vines. The large creature writhed in pain, and its body struck the side of the pit. Brightman stumbled as the ground shook again, and then continued to move forward. He ran past the burning vine like appendages and made it to the opening at the end of the walkway. He stared at the edge, fear and paranoia paralyzing his movements. The walkway opened into a large area with a steep drop-off.

Brightman stood high above the ground that offered escape and swayed at the edge. Ashley slowly moved toward Brightman, covering the ground in front of her with flame. The fire kept the vines from grabbing both of them. She moved until her back was tight against Brightman's back. She used her flame gun to cover the area around them in walls of fire. The creature roared again, and its large head lunged into the side of the pit. Brightman lost his balance and fell off the edge of the walkway into the area below. His body twisted and bounced against the ground during his long tumble to the bottom. Ashley turned around and jumped off. She used the side of the cliff area as a ramp and slid down. The heavy rain caused the ground to soften, like mud. Vines followed her, trying to grab her body and pull her to the large mass that shuddered violently behind her. Ashley traveled down the mud slide and crashed into Brightman when she hit the bottom. She pushed him forward and sent flames up the side they had fallen from. The flame gun created a high wall of fire at least six or seven feet tall. At the top of the cliff the large head of the creature roared, peering at Ashley with its piercing yellow eyes.

"Into the forest," shouted Ashley. "Brightman, go now, into the forest."

Brightman pulled himself to his feet and struggled toward the forest ahead. The scattered green grass and mud opened up into a grassy field that gave way to a line of pine trees. Brightman crashed into the tree line. The pine needles smacked his face. He put up his arms and stumbled ahead. He continued to move forward for what felt like an eternity. Finally, he broke through the dense tree line and a small clearing opened up. He turned around and watched the tree line part as Ashley stumbled through, smoke billowing into the sky behind her. The clearing allowed little sunlight to poke through. Brightman could still hear the creature roaring behind them. Ashley motioned to Brightman and they moved deeper into the forest, away from the mass grave.

Ashley and Brightman stumbled on for a few more minutes and then stopped to catch their breath.

"I think we're safe now," said Ashley as she doubled over, out of breath.

"Yeah, but where are we?" asked Brightman. "And where did these trees come from?"

Ashley remained silent. Her jumpsuit was soaked from the wet mud, and her face was covered as well. "I don't know," she replied, "but let's keep moving. That Marrow Muncher is still too close for comfort."

Brightman walked over to Ashley and wiped the mud from her face. "Thanks," he said.

"For what?" asked Ashley.

"For getting us out of there," said Brightman.

"I was more worried about myself," said Ashley.

Brightman put his head down and then laughed slightly. "Have you seen trees like this before?"

Ashley looked into the pine forest and paused. "No, these are definitely new."

Brightman nodded and decided to start walking again. Ashley soon caught up to him, and they began to navigate the dark pine forest. Silence surrounded them save for their random footsteps on broken branches. Night began to close in around them just as they reached the edge of the forest. In front of them, a clearing opened up. The ground was covered in a heavy growth of green grass, and various yellow flowers peeked through the thick, heavy grass canvas. Brightman noticed smoke rising into the sky in the distance.

"Look at that," said Ashley.

Brightman looked away from the smoke and saw the large gate of red light stretch across the open area. "Are those stealth lights?"

"I think so," replied Ashley.

Brightman walked forward and put his hand through the beams of red light.

"I've never seen a gate that big before," said Ashley.

"I wouldn't do that if I were you," shouted a voice in the distance.

Brightman took a step back and looked at Ashley in disbelief. "Who said that?" he yelled.

"I know who you are," boomed the voice "but I don't know your lady friend. Tell her to put down her duffel bag and drop the fire stick."

"I'm not doing anything until you tell me who you are!" yelled Brightman.

"Fine," bellowed the voice, "we'll do this the hard way."

A gunshot resounded in the air and struck the ground a few feet away from Brightman. "Tell your lady friend to put down her gear."

Ashley set down the duffel bag and flame unit and raised her hands in the air. "It's okay, Brightman."

Brightman followed Ashley's lead and put his arms in the air.

"I'm going to send someone to get you," the voice said. "I wouldn't try to move. You've activated a minefield. One wrong step—and *boom*."

A rustling sound, faint at first, began to grow louder, and a dark shape on four legs walked toward Brightman and Ashley.

"What's that?" asked Ashley, growing nervous and glancing toward her flame unit.

"It's a dog," said Brightman. "Haven't you ever seen a dog?"

"No," replied Ashley. "Are they dangerous?"

"That depends," said Brightman.

The dog shambled into view. Attached to its back was a makeshift harness, and it pulled a medium-size cart behind it. The dog walked up to Ashley, sniffed her, and then sat down. Its floppy ears lazily settled around a large head attached to a thick body.

"What is it doing?" asked Ashley.

"It's smelling you," said Brightman.

"How do you know it's a dog?" asked Ashley. "And how do you know what it is if you don't have any memories?"

"I don't know," said Brightman. "I just do."

"Well, I don't like it," said Ashley. "Its eyes look dangerous."

"The dog is a she, not an it, and her name is Annie," boomed the voice, "and she is dangerous. She can rip you into shreds if she wants. Now slowly put your gear into the cart."

Ashley peered at Annie and watched the chocolate-covered dog sit quietly near her feet. Brightman carefully put the duffel bag in the cart and motioned for Ashley to do the same with her flame unit. Ashley cast a sideways glance toward Annie and placed her flame unit in the cart.

"Bring them back, Annie," the mysterious voice boomed from an unseen perch.

Annie turned around and walked toward the voice carrying the gear in the cart with ease. Her strong legs walked at a quick pace.

"What are you two waiting for?" the voice asked. "Follow Annie."

Brightman nodded to Ashley and they walked behind the dog. "Minefield," mumbled Brightman.

"I heard that," said the voice. "You just mind your step."

The pair followed Annie across a dense grass field until a large ranch structure appeared in view. Behind the building, large metal windmills gently twirled. The building stretched across the grass field, showing off its expanse. A few broken-down cars sat on the right side. Various worktables littered the front area of the ranch.

"That's far enough," said the voice.

Brightman and Ashley stopped moving and waited. The front door to the ranch opened, and an older man with a large gray beard stepped into view. Atop his head a dusty cowboy hat hid his balding head. The remainder of his hair was in a ponytail that dangled down his back, gray like the man's beard. The man held a long rifle in his hands. Annie walked up to him and sat down, turning to look at Brightman. A dark shirt lined with pockets covered the man's chest. On top of the shirt a tan vest with even more pockets covered the old man's slight build. Dusty gray work pants ran down to his feet, which bore dirty brown work boots.

The old man looked at Brightman with sea-blue eyes and laughed. "I never thought I'd see you again."

Ashley whispered to Brightman, "You know this guy?"

"I have no clue who he is," said Brightman.

The old man grabbed the gear from the cart pulled by Annie. He quickly detached the harness on her back and then disappeared into the ranch. Annie looked at Brightman, and her tail began wagging. She barked once and then followed the old man into the house.

"Don't just stand there," said the old man. "I mean, you can if you want to. But I have food and clean clothes in here, if you're hungry. Judging from the way you smell, a bath might suit you as well."

Brightman turned to Ashley and shrugged. They slowly walked into the ranch house.

"I've been waiting for you for a long time, John Brightman," said the old man.

THE SIGNAL

Bird and Jessup trudged through the heavy rainfall. Every so often Bird would stop and scan the area behind them for someone or something following them. Her scans never turned up any life forms, but a slight paranoia crept into her thoughts, making her uneasy. They stopped when they needed to in order to change Leaf and make sure he ate. Leaf remained fairly quiet as Bird and Jessup pushed on through the rain. They walked until daybreak and then decided to rest. Jessup scouted out an old camper that offered modest accommodations from the rain and creatures that might wander the area.

Jessup sat in a mold-covered chair, giving the remains of a dilapidated bed to Bird and Leaf. Bird removed her helmet and gently removed Leaf from his makeshift carrier. She let her hair down, and it fell around her shoulders and onto Leaf's head. Jessup removed his heavy backpack and looked at Bird. "Any luck with the signal?" he asked.

Bird kissed Leaf on the forehead and stared out the small window of the camper. "I think we are almost there," she said. "I want to rest here and travel more when night falls. I think we should be able to reach the source in another hour or two."

"Isn't it safer to travel during the day?" asked Jessup.

"I don't know who or what is responsible for the signal, Jessup," said Bird. "We can use the cover of night to scout the area a bit."

"Makes sense," said Jessup. "Leaf is quiet, all things considered."

"He gets that from his father," said Bird.

"What was he like?" asked Jessup, "Leaf's father."

Bird didn't answer right away. She bounced Leaf softly on her chest, and he giggled slightly. The rain began to let up until only scant drops randomly bounced off the roof of the camper. "He was a strong man," said Bird, speaking slowly. "He held strong convictions. Something bothered him about the underground—enough that he refused to return."

"I've never been to the underground," said Jessup. "I've heard stories, though."

Bird remained silent as her thoughts drifted to Bear. The conversation made her feel slightly uncomfortable. "I try not to think about it anymore," she said.

"Sorry," said Jessup. "I didn't mean to pry. I don't know much about my parents. The people at the dam found me when I was young. It's all very hazy. Do you think anyone survived the attack?"

"I don't know, Jessup," said Bird. "Regardless, I'm not going back. Leaf needs to get some sleep and so do I. I suggest you try as well, Jessup."

Jessup nodded and curled into the moldy, flattened cushions of the chair. He cast an eye toward Bird one last time until sleep crept in. Bird's long blond hair shined in the faint rays of light that lit up the camper. She gently placed Leaf on the bed and sat with her back against the camper's rusty wall. Her last thoughts danced with her through sleep. Dreams of Bear filled her soul and carried her subconscious into a state of peace.

Bird awoke a few hours later. Night had replaced the day. The temperature had dropped a bit and Bird tended to Leaf when he began to cry. Jessup awoke a short time later. He noticed that Bird was gone from her bed. He stepped outside the camper and saw her scanning the distance with her helmet. The ground around the camper sprouted grass in a circular area about three feet out. He knelt down and touched the grass with his fingers.

"There is a structure northeast of here," said Bird as she pointed into the night. "Grab your gear. It's time to go, Jessup."

Jessup nodded and went back into the camper and secured his backpack. He kept the phase pistol at the ready in its holster. Jessup joined Bird and Leaf, and they made their way to the source of the signal. They traveled in silence until the outlines of a structure became visible. Bird's helmet cast a gentle blue light in the night. Broken walls lined the outskirts of the area. Within the walls sat a larger two-story building. A tower stood to the right of the complex with access through a hallway off the main building. The area's shape gave the look of an old air base. Bird motioned to Jessup, and the two slowly entered through a hole in one of the tall walls.

"Look," whispered Jessup as he pointed to a window in the second story of the structure. "Do you see the light in the window?"

Bird nodded and quickly scanned the area. "I'm getting one life form reading. It's human."

"Well, that's good," said Jessup. "Better than one of those monsters."

Bird silently drew her katana and walked toward the building. Jessup took his phase pistol from its holster and quietly followed Bird. They navigated through the shadows and made their way to a door. Bird tried the lock, but it wouldn't give.

"Hold on," said Jessup as he holstered his pistol and retrieved thieves' tools from his pocket. After a minute or so the lock opened.

Bird looked at Jessup quizzically and then proceeded through the door. She moved slowly down a hall and motioned to a large room. Old tables and chairs took up most of the space, and broken vending machines lay near the sides of the room, their food long since gone. Jessup and Bird moved out of the room and farther down the hall. Large stairs opened up in front of them. Bird cautiously walked up toward a wooden door. Jessup watched their back with his pistol. Bird reached the top of the stairs and pushed open a rotting door. A medium-sized room with an old fireplace in the far wall greeted Bird and Jessup. A healthy fire burned and offered heat for Bird's cold bones.

"This is the room I must have seen the light in," said Jessup.

Bird moved across the room to another door. She pressed on it, and the rusty metal door swung open. Jessup followed close behind Bird. They entered the room. A cot lay in the corner, its old ragged blankets cast off to one side. Moldy magazines lined the floors, and pictures covered the walls. Bird looked at the pictures and noticed they bore a resemblance to some of the magazines Bear had shown her.

"Don't move," said a stern female voice from behind Jessup and Bird.

Jessup turned around and saw the figure of a slight woman standing in the light cast by the fireplace. She held a phase rifle with a fully charged energy cell. The gun was pointed straight at Jessup. "Um, Bird," said Jessup.

Bird turned around and looked at the strange woman. Long black hair rested on her shoulders. She wore army fatigues and black boots. A large knife shined in the firelight attached to her belt. The woman's skin appeared leathery from exposure to the sun, and brown eyes stared back at Bird.

"I said don't move. Why did you move? Never mind! Drop your weapons," said the woman, motioning with her phase rifle. "I don't want to hurt you, but I will."

Jessup slowly lowered his phase pistol and placed it by his feet. Bird hesitated a moment and then lowered her katana. Leaf began whimpering.

"Is that a baby?" asked the woman.

"Yes," said Jessup. "We mean you no harm."

"I'll be the judge of that," said the woman. "Kick your weapons over to me. Slowly."

Jessup gently kicked his pistol away. Bird placed her katana on the floor and hesitantly kicked it toward their assailant. The woman holding her rifle pointed it at Bird and Jessup and picked up their weapons, tossing them to the corner of the large room. "Slowly, back out of the room. Don't make any quick moves or I'll shoot you. I swear I will."

Jessup nodded and motioned toward Bird to do the same. "Slowly," said the woman.

Bird and Jessup complied with the stranger. She held them at gunpoint and forced them into a room down the hall from the main room. She closed the strong metal door and spoke through the door. "You are going to stay there until I figure out what to do with you."

"We come from the west, the dam," said Jessup. "We are fleeing an attack."

Bird sat down against the wall of the room, holding Leaf tightly against her chest. His cries filled the empty and windowless room. "Now what?" asked Jessup as he banged his fist against the metal door.

"You are going to sit there until my friends come back," replied the woman's voice. "Now shut up! I have a headache."

Jessup sat across from Bird, his shoulders slumped. "Great," he mumbled.

Bird remained silent and kept to herself. Time seemed to stand still. She wasn't quite sure how many hours passed. Then she began to scream, "My baby, my baby! Something is wrong."

"I'm not going to fall for that!" shouted the woman. "Now, I said shut up or I'll come in there and shut you up for good!"

Jessup looked at Bird and began to scream. "The baby has stopped breathing. Help us, please!"

Bird continued screaming and sobbing nonstop. Her screams filled the woman's head. "I said shut up!"

The door burst open, and the woman appeared, pointing her gun toward Bird. "Shut up or I'll kill you right now. Baby or not!"

Bird quickly tapped her wrist device, activating a tachyon pulse. The light around her exploded in purple and red waves of energy. Adrenaline coursed through Bird's body. Moving at a blinding speed, she struck the woman in the face with a clenched fist, sending her sprawling into the corner. The rifle fell to the ground, and the woman crumbled in a heap. The light enveloping Bird faded, and her statuesque form returned to view. "Find something to tie her up!" shouted Bird.

Jessup nodded and rummaged the area. He found some ripped clothing and fastened the woman's arms tightly behind her back. "I know these rags," said Jessup. "They're from the scout teams sent from the dam."

Bird walked over to the woman. She opened her eyes again and laughed. "My friends won't be as kind as I was. I should have just killed you both when I saw you."

Bird picked up her katana and struck the woman in the face with the end of the hilt. The woman fell back into unconsciousness. "Why did you do that?" asked Jessup.

"I didn't want to hear her squawking," said Bird as she pulled the woman by her feet into the room they had just escaped, and shut the heavy steel door. "We need to move fast," she said to Jessup. "She mentioned she has friends."

Jessup nodded and picked up his phase pistol. "Right," he said. "So now what?"

"Look around the rest of the area. We will wait for her friends to come back," said Bird. Jessup nodded and headed into the structure to see what he could find.

Jessup navigated the building, which held more rooms than he first thought. The winding hallways and empty areas didn't offer much. Jessup felt content in his search until he found a trapdoor. He barely noticed it at first. It wasn't until red streaks and crimson stains led his eye to the opening. Jessup pulled on the latch and the door opened. The room below appeared dark, so Jessup turned on his flashlight. Steps led into a small basement area. Various hooks hung from the ceiling, and two large tables sat against the back wall. Metal buckets rested on top of the tables. Jessup peered into a bucket and saw pounds of red flesh. The meat looked unusual to Jessup. The room stank of death and made Jessup gag once or twice. Near the side of the table sat a pile of bloodstained clothes. Jessup looked through the clothes and noticed the scout team insignia on a sleeve similar to the ties he had used to bind the woman Bird had knocked out. To the left of the clothes an opening in the wall stood out to Jessup. He shined his light in the hole and noticed gear belonging to the scout teams.

The smell began to overpower Jessup, and he hunched over, vomiting onto the blood-caked floor. He noticed various knives and tools used by a butcher, covered in pieces of flesh. Jessup wiped bits of vomit from his mouth and left the room, aghast at his discovery.

Bird met Jessup in a lower hall. Sweat dripped from his brow. "I, I think I found the members of the scout team that never returned to the dam."

"What are you talking about?" asked Bird.

"The people here," said Jessup. "I think the people here are cannibals."

"Are you sure?" asked Bird.

"Yes," replied Jessup.

Bird gripped the hilt of her katana in anger and headed back to the room where they kept the woman. Leaf grew agitated and began to cry. Bird lowered the scarlet wrap over his eyes and pulled open the door to the room holding the woman. "I want some answers," said Bird, standing in front of her captive while pointing the katana toward the woman's chest.

Bird's prisoner watched Jessup stumble into view. His complexion was ghost white, and sweat covered his face. "You found the room," the woman. She laughed. "No matter: my friends will be back soon."

Bird pressed the katana's sharp tip against the woman's chest, drawing blood. "The signal you use?" asked Bird.

"It's an old signal we put on loop," the woman said, laughing again. "Helps draw people near."

"Why?" asked Bird, pressing the katana harder against the woman's chest.

"Why do people do anything in this world?" asked the woman. "We did what we needed to in order to survive. You would do the same if you had to protect your child."

Bird withdrew the blade from her chest and stepped back. "I would never do what you have done! How many friends are coming back?"

"You'll find out soon enough," the woman said. "Are you so sure you wouldn't do anything to protect your child?"

A large explosion bellowed from downstairs, and smoke began to creep into the room. "Looks like you are going to find out right now. They will enjoy your flesh. We liked the taste. Oh, we so liked the taste." The woman licked her lips and laughed.

Bird raised her katana in the air and slashed across the woman's throat. The blade easily cut through her flesh, sending the woman's head rolling to the side of her motionless body. Blood spilled out onto the floor. Bird pushed the corpse aside and walked out of the room into the smoke. Blue light shined through the smoke from her helmet and outlined the area in front of Bird.

"Get to the tower, Jessup, and lock yourself inside," shouted Bird. "Don't open the door no matter what. If I don't come for you, Jessup, do not let yourself be taken alive. Do you understand?"

Jessup nodded and covered his nose and mouth from the smoke. He ran through the hallways and disappeared, heeding Bird's instructions.

Bird went back down the stairs and entered the large room she and Jessup had found earlier, withdrawing into the shadows. Three large outlines moved past the room through the smoke. Bird scanned behind them and noticed a fourth. Bird waited until the fourth passed the doorway and grabbed the figure by its head. Bird felt a bone mask and discerned that the figure was male. She quickly raised her katana and cut the man's throat open. He gurgled for a moment as his lifeblood spilled onto the floor. Bird moved quickly, following the remaining assailants. She made her way back up the stairs and saw another man hunched over the body of the woman Bird had beheaded earlier. She moved swiftly and shoved her katana deep into the man's body. Her hand covered his mouth, and he fell to the floor.

"Did you hear that?" asked another man.

"Yeah, go check it out," another replied. "I saw someone head toward the tower."

The man nodded to his friend and headed back to the room with the fireplace. He noticed the outline of a slender figure moving through the smoke, and then the unforgiving steel of a katana pierced his flesh. Bird moved angrily and pushed the man against the wall, holding his mouth with her hand as the katana dug into his midsection. "Shhhhh," whispered Bird as her katana made its final lethal thrust.

Bird lowered the scarlet cover farther over Leaf's head and chased after the last man. She rounded the corner and saw the door to the tower kicked open. The man, standing well over six feet tall, adorned in bones from creatures and pieces of metal arranged to form makeshift armor, held Jessup by the neck. The man raised a pistol to Jessup's head. Bird clicked another tachyon pulse and jumped forward into the kaleidoscope of swirling colors. Her katana struck the man in the back, and she pulled the blade upward. Blood spattered Jessup's face. Bird could see the man's finger pulling the trigger to the pistol in his death throes. Still within the tachyon pulse Bird nudged the man's hand that held the gun, and the shot went off, grazing Jessup's side as the tachyon pulse faded.

The man's heavy body fell onto Jessup, covering him in blood. Bird withdrew her katana and pushed the dead man from atop Jessup. "Are you all right?" asked Bird.

Jessup sat in silence, rubbed the side of his temple, and looked up at Bird. "How did you do that?"

"I'll explain later," Bird replied.

Bird and Jessup spent the remainder of the night dragging the bodies into the open area behind the air base. They set the dead ablaze and watched the flames engulf the cannibals' bodies. "I would rather have buried them and left them for the creatures," said Bird.

"Aye," said Jessup. "They don't deserve honor in death."

Bird watched Jessup throw the pile of rags that had belonged to the scout party from the dam into the flames. She didn't say anything as he lowered his head and watched the rags turn to ash in the fading night sky. Bird peered down at Leaf as he slept quietly in the shadow of the burning flames. She noticed that her light blue jumpsuit wore the blood of the cannibals she had slain. Their lifeblood was a stain on her clothes, providing a stark reminder of the horrors the world contains. As the last of the fires burned out, Bird remembered the words of the woman. They remained in her mind as she gently kissed Leaf on his head.

SOMETHING BEGINS
TO GROW

Jessup spent the next few days cleaning up the reminders of the previous occupants that had made their home in the air base. He cleaned up most of the debris and set up a makeshift nursery for Bird and Leaf. There wasn't much left from the equipment of the scout teams the cannibals had killed. Jessup found a few stray ration cubes but nothing else. What he found in the lower levels near the trapdoor surprised him the most. He decided to see if Bird had woken up for the day. She had slept heavily the previous few days, and Jessup had dutifully tended to Leaf as she slept.

Jessup opened the door to Bird's room slowly. He carried Leaf the best he could in his thin arms. Leaf began crying loudly for the tender embrace of his mother. Bird rolled over in the makeshift bed and opened her eyes.

"Ah good," said Jessup, walking over to Bird. "I think someone missed you."

Bird smiled and nestled Leaf in her bosom. Her jumpsuit hung in the corner of the room, and Bird wore a scant tattered white dress Jessup had found in the debris. She glanced toward her jumpsuit and noticed the bloodstains had faded.

"I cleaned up your suit a little," said Jessup as he opened a ripped curtain on the far window to allow sunlight to enter the room.

"Thank you," said Bird, rising from her bed and walking over to the window. She peered into the distance. The area surrounding the base was made up of dirt covered in red dust. A few sickly trees stretched out for sunlight, but their pleas went unanswered as purple and red clouds rolled in and covered the nourishing light.

"I've been cleaning up the air base since you've been sleeping, and tending to Leaf," said Jessup.

"How long have I been sleeping?" asked Bird, walking away from the window and placing Leaf in a tiny box crib that Jessup had made.

"A few days," replied Jessup. "I found something. That's why I checked to see if you were awake."

Bird pulled back her hair and put her arms around her body to stave off a chill that lingered in the air. "What did you find?" asked Bird.

"A supply room," said Jessup. "A room full of food, fuel, water, clothes, blankets, and just about anything you could want."

Bird's eyes lit up and she smiled at Jessup. "That's great, Jessup!"

"I don't understand why the people here turned to cannibalism with all this," Jessup said faintly.

Bird thought of the Black Mist she had encountered that had consumed Fox. "I don't know, Jessup," she said. "This world. Something in it makes people do vile things." Bird paused for a moment and decided not to inform Jessup about the Black Mist she had witnessed months earlier.

"There is more," Jessup said, smiling. "The radio signal. I figured out how to get it off the loop. We can record a message. I don't fully understand it, but most of it's working. So, do you have anything you want to say to the world?"

"Me?" asked Bird.

"Yes, you," replied Jessup. "All you have to do is record a message and we can send it out."

Leaf let out a cry, and Bird retrieved him from his makeshift crib. She pushed aside her white dress a bit and allowed the babe to mouth her breast. Jessup blushed a bit and turned his head. "So, should we record a message?"

Bird smiled. "Yes. I don't know what I'll say, but I'll do it."

"Great," said Jessup. "Let's go."

Jessup quickly walked out of the room and headed toward the tower. Bird followed Jessup until they arrived at the destination. The tower had low walls, and the top area showcased four large glass panels that offered a view onto the desolate wasteland below. "See that building over there?" asked Jessup.

Bird nodded, and sat down in the chair Jessup pointed to. "Yes," said Bird.

"There is a plane inside. One of those older fighter jets. It's damaged pretty badly," said Jessup. "Never mind that. Here: speak into this when you're ready, and we'll send a message."

Jessup handed Bird a microphone and flipped a switch. He nodded to her. Bird cleared her throat and began to speak. "Hello. My name is Bird. I am with good people here. We have food and shelter from the dangers of the surface. I am from part of a recon group formerly of the Pacific base. We fled the underground in hopes of finding a life above the surface. I am sending this message in the belief that it will reach someone out there."

Bird stepped back from the microphone. "How did I do?"

"Sounded good to me," said Jessup. "Hey, there is something else."

"What is it, Jessup?" asked Bird.

"That day we slept in the camper, remember?" asked Jessup.

"I remember," said Bird. "Why?"

"The night we left, I noticed small bits of grass growing around the outside of the camper," said Jessup. "I didn't think anything about it until I noticed this."

Jessup motioned to Bird, and then he left the tower and headed to the perimeter of the base. He opened a door to the outside and pointed at the ground. "Look."

Bird knelt down and touched the light green grass that sprouted up from the red-dust-covered ground. The grass felt cold to her touch but soft and soothing. "I don't understand," she said.

"It's all around the perimeter of the base," said Jessup, scratching his head. "Back at the dam it took weeks or months to grow stuff. This sprouted up in a few days."

Bird pulled Leaf closer to her chest and shivered as a cold breeze cut through her scant dress. "Let's go back inside. It's getting damp."

Jessup nodded, and they returned inside. "I'll build a fire," said Jessup.

Bird sat in a musty chair that Jessup placed in the room with the fireplace. He cleaned the splattered blood of the cannibals from the walls and started a small fire. He reached to a pile of old pictures, books, and magazines. Jessup grabbed an old picture and went to toss it into the tiny flame. "No, not that," said Bird.

"This? It's just some old picture," said Jessup.

"Please, Jessup," said Bird. "Find something else to burn."

"All right," replied Jessup. He exited the room and returned with a torn suitcase. Large piles of money lined the inside. Jessup grabbed a few handfuls and tossed the bills into the fire. "I guess this stuff isn't any good anymore."

Bird sat back in the chair and watched the money burn in the flames. She looked at Leaf's head and noticed more hair had grown in, in bright white. She covered his visible hair with the scarlet wrap and chuckled as the flames engulfed the currency.

"We would be rich if this stuff still held any value," said Jessup as he looked at the old picture Bird had told him not to burn. The picture showed a group of people sitting in a grass field. A bright yellow sun cast its light throughout the sky surrounded by a blue canvas dotted with white clouds. The people looked happy, thought Jessup.

"Do you think anyone will respond to our message?" asked Jessup, tossing more money into the flames.

"I don't know, Jessup," replied Bird. "I don't know …"

"With our luck, maybe it would be better if nobody did," said Jessup.

WE SHOULD
PROBABLY LEAVE

E d listened to his superior go through the standard debriefing after every mission. Most of what the inquisitor told Ed ended up being Elder-PC-speak until he asked about Jones. Ed related his side of what had happened. He told his superior that Jones had left the immediate area to pursue a fleeing cult member. When Ed had found his body, the cult members scattered. "From what I gather, a cult member or members overpowered Jones and shot him with his pistol. The entire encounter didn't end up friendly," said Ed, shifting in his chair a bit. "I made that very clear in the report. I instructed my team not to use live rounds."

"I am aware of what happened, Ed," said his superior. "I commend you for trying to have the incident end peacefully, but these are trying times. The people of the common seem to respond only to force."

Ed bit his tongue and remained silent. *Maybe if the Elders didn't treat them like rats*, he thought. He shifted again in the rigid chair and looked around the bland office of his interrogator.

"Unless you have anything else to add, I will file this away," said his superior.

"No," said Ed. "That's all I have to add."

"Thank you, Edward," said his superior. "You will receive the standard two days of rest and recuperation. You are dismissed."

Ed got up from the chair and walked out of the debriefing room. He hated going through those interrogations. At least they didn't selectively wipe your mind after a recon mission. *Two days of rest and recuperation,* he thought. *Might as well get my pick-me-up from the doc's refilled and return to my drug-induced haze.* The line at the doctor's moved quickly, and Ed picked up his prescription without much ado and headed back to his hole in the wall to think. People stayed off the streets, and some shops still kept their doors closed. After an incident like the one that had just happened, most people got a bit edgy. Ed wondered if the tactics of the riot squad actually helped. *Maybe I'm on the wrong side of all of this,* he thought. His hands haphazardly fumbled with his entry key to his room. Then he noticed a yellow rag stuck on the door handle.

"Oh, shit," mumbled Ed.

Yanti and Ed had a system. If there happened to be any sort of trouble, Yanti would place a yellow rag on Ed's door. The system used a color-coded threat indicator. Yellow, unfortunately, happened to be the worst. Ed quickly entered his room and walked over to his small storage area. He pushed away a pile of junk and pressed a hidden latch that opened a panel in the floor. Ed grabbed a phase pistol, dark sunglasses, a COMM unit, and a mini EMP device from the inside of the compartment. He quickly put on his black Hawaiian shirt, blue jeans, and black sneakers.

"Ed," said Lesly. "Ed, you left the door open. I've come by to drop off your stuff."

Ed quickly turned around and pulled Lesly into the room and shut the door. "Did anyone follow you?" asked Ed. "Does anyone know you are here?"

"I finished my shift at the station," said Lesly. "I mentioned I was going to see you."

"Shit!" mumbled Ed.

"You are acting really weird, Ed," said Lesly. "Even weirder than you normally do."

Ed pushed Lesly back and slowly inched his door open. He peered through the tiny crack and noticed a few burly men wearing yellow armor approaching from the alley. The lead man made an arm motion, and two others aimed their weapons toward Ed's door.

"Just do what I say!" shouted Ed. "Just trust me."

Ed grabbed Lesly and dived over the small bed in his room. Gunshots exploded against the door and pushed the metal off its hinges. A loud thud followed, and the door flew across the room. Ed flipped the mattress over, carrying it like a shield, and ran toward the door. He crashed into the men, knocking them down with his weight behind the mattress. He sprang up quickly and fired off multiple shots with his phase pistol into the mattress that lay atop the men. The mattress soaked up the blood from the gunshot wounds.

"What did you just do?" screamed Lesly.

Ed put his sunglasses on, an older style of aviator shades he had found on the surface, and grabbed Lesly by the hand. "We need to go right now!" he shouted.

Lesly teetered in her high heels and decided to just toss them off. "If I had known we were going to be chased by people, I would have dressed differently," shouted Lesly. "This is so typical of you, Ed."

Ed looked over at Lesly and mused over her clingy light green dress, high heels, and long dirty-blond hair that dangled past her shoulders. She had even put a few subtle pink highlights in.

"Just follow me and keep moving," said Ed. "Hopefully Yanti is all right."

"Who is Yanti?" asked Lesly. "What have you gotten yourself into?"

"No time to explain," said Ed. "I'm sorry you are involved. They know you saw me. They won't let you go now."

"Who won't let me go?" asked Lesly.

"The Elders," said Ed.

"The Elders!" shouted Lesly. "I should turn you in myself."

"Ashley is in trouble," said Ed.

"Ashley," said Lesly. "Figures it was like you were married to her and not me. Typical."

Ed pulled Lesly close to him and pushed her up against the wall. "Kiss me," said Ed.

"No, I'm not going kiss you," said Lesly.

Ed glanced over his shoulder and kissed his wife against the wall of a common's alley. A few guards walked down the street. One turned toward the two and then moved on. "You don't want to get the Rot," said one of his fellow guards. "Let's move."

The guards disappeared down the narrow street, and Ed withdrew his mouth from his wife's. "Just like old times," said Ed. "C'mon this way. The archives are up here."

"Don't flatter yourself, Edward," said Lesly. "You aren't a very good kisser."

"I'm probably a better kisser than that guy you are with now—what's his name?" asked Ed.

"Leave him out of this," said Lesly. "He works hard and doesn't have half the military chasing after him."

"We're here," said Ed.

Ed motioned to Lesly to walk ahead. He approached the door to the archives and hit the buzzer. "Yanti," said Ed. "Yanti, let me in."

"Who's the broad?" asked Yanti.

"She's with me," said Ed. "Are you going to let us in or not?"

The door buzzed and slipped open. Ed and Lesly entered quickly, and the door slammed shut behind them, locking instantly. "Yanti, we don't have time for games," said Ed. "Where are you?"

"I'm down here," said Yanti.

Ed looked around and saw Yanti moving a few air tanks around in an underground room. "When did you put that room in?" asked Ed.

"This is a last-ditch plan, Ed," said Yanti. "You really stepped into some shit this time."

"What else is new," snipped Lesly, rolling her eyes.

"I could use a hand, you know," said Yanti, "instead of you just standing there."

Ed jumped into the underground area. Yanti finished zipping up a wet suit and adjusted an air tank on his back. "You are lucky, Ed," said Yanti. "I have enough wet suits for everyone."

"Wet suits," said Lesly. "Whoa—you mean like swimming-in-the-tank wet suits. Oh no. No way."

Yanti tossed a wet suit toward Ed. "Put it on, and fast. I don't know who you are, lady, but in a few minutes this place is going to be crawling with goons."

"My name is Lesly Cole," said Lesly.

"Hey, Ed, isn't that your last name?" asked Yanti.

"Yes," said Ed.

"So you two, what are you, married?" asked Yanti.

"Divorced," piped Lesly, growing irritated.

"You never filed the paperwork," said Ed.

"Argue later, you two," barked Yanti.

Lesly reluctantly lowered herself into the room and took a wet suit from Yanti. She struggled with it a bit before Ed helped her zip it up and fasten the air tank to her back. "We can exit through there," said Yanti, pointing to a latch on the far wall. "There is an air lock. All we need to do is swim about a hundred yards to a junction and we can get back inside."

"I know that junction," said Ed. "From there we can go to the old jump line. It's not far."

"You mean jump as in jump to the surface," said Lesly. "Are you crazy?"

"A few days ago, I would have said he is definitely crazy," said Yanti. "There is some heavy shit going on right now. The info I picked for you, Ed, had tracking scripts like I've never seen. Someone doesn't want you sniffing around. That's not the worst part. That Sub Blackness cult you sniffed out? They are planning something big. An attack."

"We should probably leave," said Ed. "We can use the old tank units to make the jump. The tanks are old, but you can probably rig something, Yanti."

"There isn't a piece of technology I can't fix or hack," said Yanti. "You know that, Ed."

Ed reached into his pocket before zipping up the wet suit and handed Yanti and Lesly tiny earpieces. "Put these in your ear," said Ed. "We'll be able to communicate while in the tank and if we get separated."

"This is crazy," said Lesly.

Ed fixed the breathing helmet on Lesly's face and turned on her air. "Can you hear me?" asked Ed.

"Yeah," said Lesly.

"Good. I'll go first. You stay between Yanti and me," said Ed as he fastened his breathing device.

Yanti handed Ed a spear gun. "I've only got the one."

Ed looked at the weapon and cringed. A bit of rust covered the tip of the spear. "Does this still work?"

Yanti gave a thumbs-up and opened the latch. Ed dropped down, followed by Lesly and then Yanti, who closed the latch behind him. Ed looked back at his companions and began turning the handle to open the air lock. A pinkish water began to fill the room. In a matter of seconds, the fluid engulfed the air lock. "Mic check," said Ed.

Yanti and Lesly gave him a thumbs-up, and the three proceeded into the tank. "Switch on your stealth units," said Ed. "The button on the top right of your mask."

Yanti and Lesly followed Ed's instructions, and a red cone of light projected from their masks. Ed clicked his, and the light flickered before turning off. He banged his mask once or twice, but the light failed to turn on. "Shit," said Ed. "Stay close to the wall of the structure. Your red light will hide you from the creatures."

"What about you, Ed?" asked Lesly.

"Just stay close to the structure," said Ed. "I'll be fine." Ed gripped the spear gun and tried to remain focused. He placed his wrist through the leather loop at the end of the spear gun.

The trio swam quickly and carefully along the side of the structure. Ed peered into the depths of the tank and didn't see anything. He couldn't see far into the liquid but remained hopeful that the base's red light system still functioned properly in this sector of the common.

As the group progressed toward the junction, a blast reverberated from within the base and shook the outside walls. Shock waves rolled through the tank, sending Lesly careening into the depths. "Ed!" screamed Lesly.

Ed reached out and grabbed Lesly's leg. "I've got you."

Lesly's momentum almost sent Ed tumbling into the tank. He grasped a handle on the side of the structure with one hand and held onto Lesly with his other. His grip slipped slightly, and then he moved his hand farther up her leg. Lesly began to panic and started kicking her legs. Ed let go of the spear gun. It floated in the tank, still attached to his wrist via the leather loop.

"Calm down," said Ed. "I've got you, but you need to stop moving."

Lesly regained her senses and stopped her frantic kicking. Ed began to pull her back to the side of the structure. "See," said Ed. "I told you I've got you."

"What was that, Yanti?" asked Ed.

"You didn't think I would let those goons get their hands on my stuff, did you?" Yanti asked, laughing.

"Unfortunately, that blast may attract some unwanted guests," said Ed.

"What kind of guests?" asked Lesly.

"You don't want to know," said Ed. "Keep moving. We are almost there."

They were about twenty yards from the junction when Ed heard the screeching. "Shit!" he shouted. "Just keep moving. Don't look!"

Ed motioned with his hand for Lesly and Yanti to continue toward the junction. He looked into the depths of the tank and saw a series of triangular creatures with tentacles trailing from their backs heading his way. The triangular head opened to reveal a series of teeth and small feelers. The creatures rushed toward Ed. He dodged the first two that approached, and they stuck onto the outer wall of the base. A third had him in its sights. Ed leveled the spear gun and fired into the monster. The creature fell away into the tank, twisting in pain. Another series of creatures approached. Ed braced for impact with the monsters. Ed watched as his friends made their way to the junction and began going inside. That's when a low rumbling emerged from the depths of the tank. The small creatures heading toward Ed scattered in the presence of the large shadow.

"Oh fuck," mumbled Ed as an enormous creature swam past him. He could reach out and touch the side of the monstrosity if he wanted. Ed couldn't move. The creature swam slowly past Ed, oblivious to his presence within the tank. A few minutes passed before the creature's massive form moved on. Ed watched the enormous thing hug the side wall of the base and then head upward.

Ed could feel his heart pounding in his chest and his breathing grow rapid to the point that he almost choked on the air. Finally, the creature disappeared from view. Ed regained his wits and swam toward the junction. He turned the handle on the latch and entered the air lock. The water from the tank drained, and Ed removed his scuba gear. Yanti opened the hatch above and extended his hand to help Ed out of the air lock.

"Did you guys see it?" asked Ed.

"See what?" asked Lesly.

Ed shook his head in disbelief: he may have just witnessed the presence of a Rig. "Never mind. Let's get out of here. The old jump point isn't far."

The small group hid their wet suits in an out-of-the-way corner and made their way through a part of the underground long forgotten by the prying eyes of the Elders. The lack of human activity made traveling easy, and Ed and company reached the jump point without much fanfare. The area had once held the appearance of an old garage. A large blue-and-white vehicle sat in front of sealed blast doors. Heavy treads lined its base, and two large rocket engines sat on the rear of the vehicle. The front of the vehicle came to a point with dark blast shields covering the glass windows of the cockpit area. A compact rounded metal piece took up the space between the cockpit and rocket engines. Ed opened the door on the side, revealing a large sitting area to carry troops.

"Yanti," said Ed.

"Yeah," replied Yanti.

"Time for you to work your magic," said Ed. "I need you to get this antique up and running."

Yanti entered the vehicle and looked around at the insides and controls. "Shouldn't be too difficult."

"How long?" asked Ed.

"Two, three hours at the most," said Yanti.

"I'm counting on you," said Ed. "The sooner we get out of here, the better."

Ed left Yanti to his work and walked over to Lesly. She rummaged through lockers, looking for more practical clothing. Ed watched her toss old clothes aside until she found something that fit. Lesly slipped off her light green dress and put on a pair of thick gray pants and a black tank top. She tossed on a black tactical vest and finally a black pair of sneakers.

"Get a good look," said Lesly as she tied her sneakers.

"How long have we been married?" Ed said, chuckling.

Lesly forcefully shut the locker and sat on a bench, crossing her legs. "You really got us in the shit this time, Ed," said Lesly.

"I don't think this was all my fault," said Ed.

"It's always your fault, Edward," said Lesly. "Ever since I've known you. I honestly don't know why I married you."

"C'mon, it hasn't been that bad," said Ed. "We've had some good times."

Lesly looked at her husband and put her head down. "That's what you don't get. You never think about how I feel."

"So, you come to my quarters in high heels and a sexy dress?" asked Ed. "You can't tell me you weren't thinking of something."

"Ugh," said Lesly as she quickly got off the bench and walked away.

Ed smiled a bit and then leaned against the wall of the garage. "Some things never change,"

Lesly avoided Ed as best she could while Yanti worked on the vehicle. Silence grew, save the curses Yanti yelled as he tossed tools around the inside of the vehicle, banging metal upon metal at times. "I think I've got it," he said finally.

"Great," said Ed. "I knew you could. Strap yourselves in, guys. I'll be there in a minute."

Ed walked to the back of the garage and entered a small control room. He looked over the buttons and pressed a sequence. The garage lit up with red lights flashing and rotating. Ed quickly tied his loose black sneaker and ran into the vehicle, where he took a seat in the cockpit. He placed his aviator sunglasses on and fired up the start-up sequence.

"Wait," said Yanti. "One final touch."

Yanti produced a small figure of a woman in a hula skirt holding a guitar. He stuck the figure to the top of the control panel. He flicked the figurine and it swayed back and forth.

"What, no blue troll?" Ed said, laughing.

"That's how you are going to the surface?" asked Lesly. "A black Hawaiian shirt, sneakers, and a pair of jeans?"

"That's how I always dress for recon assignments," said Ed.

Lesly looked at Yanti and then strapped herself in with a large black harness. "At least your friend here is prepared."

Yanti looked over the black engineering vest he had procured, plus gray work pants and a heavy pair of boots. "I try," said Yanti. "Ed, see that tiny console on the right side of the control panel with the duct tape?"

"Yep," replied Ed.

"That's to override the blast doors. This first one should open with the launch sequence. When we approach, the other two push the green button marked one for the first doors and two for the second set. I had to create a remote override since I don't have the codes," said Yanti.

"Gotcha," said Ed. "Everyone ready?"

Yanti gave a thumbs-up and Lesly mumbled, "Yeah."

The rockets in the back of the vehicle clicked on very slowly until they began spewing out flame. "Disengaging safeties," said Ed. "Hold on!"

The heavy blast doors in front of Ed opened, and the vehicle rocketed through the jump tube. A hologram of the area in front appeared on the blast shield, allowing Ed to navigate the path. Ed kept hold of the controls, which resembled a flight stick, as the force from the rocket engines bore down on the vehicle's occupants.

"Approaching first set of blast doors," chimed a soft female computerized voice.

"Flip the first switch, Ed," said Yanti.

Ed moved his hand over to the button on the console Yanti had rigged, and activated it. The doors blocking the jump tube opened and the jump tank continued at a breakneck pace. The lights began to dim a bit in the vehicle. Ed punched the control panel, and everything returned to normal. "Approaching last set of blast doors," the soft female computerized voice spoke.

Ed pushed the last button. "Warning," said the computerized voice, "Override failed. Blast doors malfunction."

"Yanti!" shouted Ed.

Yanti unbuckled himself and moved toward the cockpit. The forces of the rocket engines made his movements difficult. He pushed the button again, but nothing happened.

"Yanti!" shouted Ed, his voice growing louder.

"I'm trying," said Yanti. "There—got it."

Yanti jammed a pair of pliers into the console and held down the button.

"Blast door override successful," said the computerized voice.

The last pair of doors opened, and the vehicle shot through, exiting the jump tubes and becoming airborne. The rockets on the back of the tank broke off and the vehicle began to level out, striking the surface at a tremendous speed. The thick treads kicked in and slowed the vehicle's slide. "Jump successful," chimed the computerized voice again, "Disengaging internal blast shields. Eye protection is highly recommended.'

"I'd put those helmets on if I were you guys," said Ed as the heavy blast shields on the cockpit began to slide back.

Yanti and Lesly fumbled with the awkward helmets and secured them on their heads. Sunlight broke through the glass of the cockpit and the surface became visible. "Welcome to the surface," said Ed.

Yanti and Lesly gathered around Ed and peered through the cockpit looking at the world above for the first time. "Maybe we should go back," remarked Yanti.

SCIENCE? WHO NEEDS SCIENCE?

Marybeth stood in front of her people. Six men with black hoods on their heads knelt before her, their hands and mouths bound tightly. Behind each man stood a member from the dam. Each held a pistol and pointed it toward the back of the kneeling men's heads. A large crowd stood a few feet back, heckling the men and casting menacing stares.

"As I have said, these scientists are the reason that our men's seeds are sterile," Marybeth said. "The Bird worked with them to create a disease, which killed many—your loved ones as well as mine. You remember how my husband suffered from the disease that spread through our settlement shortly after Bird's arrival. Getting rid of these men is the first step to take back our settlement. The ultimate enemy still remains: the Bird. Today is the start of our resurgence," she preached.

The crowd raised their fists to the air and began shouting. "Are you sure this is the way?" asked a lone man near the back.

"Have I not told you about the video we found?" asked Marybeth. "Have I ever lied to you?"

Loud rumblings drowned out the man, and he slunk away, head down. Marybeth walked behind the men holding the guns and turned to the crowd. "Let the cleansing begin!" she shouted.

One by one the guns went off and the scientists' bound, and gagged bodies fell to the ground. The last man with a gun hesitated. He backed away and turned to Marybeth. "I can't." he said. "I know these men. They helped us."

Marybeth walked up to the man and pulled the gun out of his hand. She turned to the last scientist and fired. "There is no room for weakness in our settlement. That is what hurt us before. We were weak to take in the Bird, and look where we are now!"

Marybeth pointed the gun at the man. "There is no place for the weak here anymore."

"What are you doing?" asked the man. "This is insane. We knew these people."

Marybeth fired the gun and the man fell over, a bullet in his forehead. The crowd grew silent and then looked around at each other.

"Fear not, my brothers and sisters," said Marybeth. "Through this cleansing we will become strong and rebuild."

The crowd began to rumble. "No more shall we be weak!" a few people said.

"Aye, it is time to take back our lives," another yelled.

"The Bird has flown east," said Marybeth. "Who will come with me to clip her wings?"

The crowd was silent for a moment. Then a few voices gave their support. "I will go!"

"Me too," replied another man. "My wife died from the disease."

A few more offered their support. Marybeth raised her hands and looked upon her flock. "Thank you," she said. "We will return with her head."

Marybeth motioned to the crowd, and they attended to the dead bodies. "We will burn their bodies at dusk. They do not deserve honor in death, but there is no sense leaving their flesh to attract more creatures."

The night sky of the settlement lit up with funeral pyres. Embers from the burning wood floated into the horizon, rising into the clouds, and the bodies soon turned to ash scattering in the barren wasteland carried by a chilling wind to the east.

Marybeth returned to her quarters and shut the door. She went over to a large metal lockbox and opened it using a key she kept around her neck. Inside, a human skull sat surrounded by dead roses. Marybeth picked up the skull and held it near her breast, caressing the smooth bone. "My dear," whispered Marybeth, "my poor dear, I will avenge your death and kill the one responsible."

105

REVELATIONS

Brightman finished washing in the water provided by Prinn Pin. The old man welcomed John and Ashley into his home. He provided water and a stove to heat it, giving Brightman his first chance to wash since he could remember. He toweled down his body and slipped into the clothes that Prinn had available: a long-sleeve gray top, jeans, blue sneakers, and a red-and-black flannel shirt. He walked over to the mirror near a sink in the room and stared at his reflection. His hair, gone from his time in the fluid mask, didn't make him happy. He rubbed the top of his head and could feel a bit of hair growing. His face carried the beginnings of a beard. Brightman ran his hand over his face and thought to keep the growth. Prinn had mentioned a dinner, so he made his way through the cramped ranch structure to the dining area. The old man kept the home crowded with odds and ends he had procured over time. Brightman sat down at a small round table and joined Ashley and Prinn.

"I've got a special treat for you two," said Prinn as he smiled at Ashley. "When is the last time you had real food?"

"What do you mean?" asked Ashley, arms folded and not particularly comfortable in her new attire. She had given up her jumpsuit for a pair of tight-fitting blue jeans and a loose-fitting black sweater along with a pair of black sneakers. Her hair flowed out behind her, its auburn color shining in the dimly lit dining area.

Prinn quickly left the room and returned holding four white plates and set three of them on the table. He placed the fourth on the floor next to Annie. She wagged her tail and quickly ate the food Prinn had prepared for his guests.

"Fish," said Prinn.

"Where did you get this?" asked Ashley.

"While you two were getting cleaned up, Annie and I went fishing," said Prinn.

"Woof," barked Annie in approval as she sat down near Prinn's feet.

"Fish?" asked Ashley. "That's impossible."

"Well, apparently not," Prinn said, laughing. "Now eat. I have to explain a few things. I apologize for the quality. Bass isn't the tastiest fish, but it's all I could engineer with what I have."

"Engineer?" asked Brightman.

"Sorry," said Prinn. "Grow. It's the only type of fish I could grow."

"In what water?" asked Ashley.

"Just eat," said Prinn, "and I'll explain after dinner."

Brightman looked at Ashley curiously and shrugged. "When in Rome."

The three sat in silence and finished the meal Prinn had prepared. Evening closed in, and Prinn gathered their plates, disappearing into the ranch. "If you would be so kind as to head into the room down the hall," Prinn said. "There are plenty of seats. We need to talk."

Brightman and Ashley hesitated slightly and then did as instructed. Annie followed the pair into a spacious room. Along the far wall, a large table covered with a series of five computer screens and wires extending seemingly everywhere garnered Brightman's attention. Ashley sat in a black leather barrel chair next to Brightman, who sat in an identical one. Behind them a large American flag covered the wall.

Annie took a seat near Ashley and then decided to plop on her side, extending her long legs across the red carpeted floor. She huffed once and rubbed her face with her front paw. Ashley looked at her with contempt and then crossed her arms.

Prinn entered the room and took a seat at the chair by the table. He powered up the computers and turned to face his guests. "You probably want answers," said Prinn.

"I would appreciate that," said Brightman.

"I told you my name already: Prinn Pin," said Prinn. "Let me get down to it. I know who you are, Brightman, because I created you."

"Excuse me?" said Brightman.

Ashley gently touched Brightman's arm, and he quieted down.

"Yes," said Prinn. "I was the lead scientist on the Observer project. It wasn't my first idea, but it was the only thing the Elders would agree on. Originally, I wanted to use my wife's discovery of cloning and organic growth to cultivate the surface. That's why you see all the grass and trees around my home."

"Wait," said Ashley. "You can make things grow on the surface?"

"In short, yes," said Prinn. "I can to a point. It's not important right now."

"Not important?" said Ashley. "We could sustain life on the surface!"

"That's what my wife and I thought as well," said Prinn. "Unfortunately the Elders rejected our work. So, I compromised and gave them the Observers."

"You mean me?" asked Brightman.

"Not just you," said Prinn, "but yeah. You were the back door. I grew the Observers in my lab and filled your minds with memories as best I could. I knew the project wouldn't work. I rigged your recording device to connect with the other Observers and gave you enough memories to bury you from the creature's detection. As the other Observers died, their recordings transferred into you. So, you have all of what they saw in your head."

"That's why the Elders wanted to bring me back—to get the information?" asked Brightman.

"I stopped trusting the Elders long ago. After I completed the project, my wife and I left the underground and came here. The Elders never wanted to destroy the original creature—whatever you call it in the underground. They wanted to control it from the very beginning," Prinn paused as he noticed Ashley shifting in her chair. "I'm sorry to tell you this, Ashley, but the Elders used you as well. Why do you think they would selectively wipe your mind after a mission?"

"I'm going to need more proof than some old coot's ramblings," said Ashley in a defensive tone.

"Wait," said Brightman. "Let him speak. How were they going to get the information out of my head?"

"You didn't tell him?" asked Prinn as he looked at Ashley.

"No," she replied. "I didn't want to jeopardize the mission."

"What are you talking about?" asked Brightman.

"The procedure to extract the recorder from your head, Brightman, would have left you a vegetable," said Prinn.

"You knew about this, Ashley?" asked Brightman, looking directly at her.

Ashley moved her hand to comfort John. "I'm sorry, but I was following orders. I—"

Brightman pushed her hand away. "No need to explain."

"I'm sorry, but you needed to know the truth," said Prinn.

Brightman sat in silence for a moment and then got up from the chair. "I need to lie down. If you will excuse me."

"John," said Ashley. "I would have told you."

"When?" asked Brightman. "After they cut up my brain? I need to think."

Prinn motioned to Ashley and she stayed seated. She watched Brightman get up and leave the room.

Brightman clenched his fists in anger and retreated to the sleeping quarters Prinn had set up for him. He shut the door and locked it, and then crawled onto the small cot in the corner. He stared blankly at the far wall until sleep crept in. The familiar blackness surrounded him. In the distance the faint machinery echoed toward him. This time the sound seemed faint. Brightman stumbled through his hell and noticed something different. Areas of the blackness seemed alight with colorful images. He couldn't discern quite what they were, but they seemed familiar and soothing. As he walked through, the dark flashes of light appeared. He decided to make his way toward a faint light in the distance. The sound of machinery grew silent, and a lighted door appeared.

"Hello," said a tiny voice.

"Who's there?" asked Brightman.

A crackling of light shined, and a small skunk sauntered into view. "Someone who wants to help," said the skunk.

"A talking skunk?" asked Brightman

"What exactly were you expecting?" asked the skunk.

"Never mind," said Brightman. "How exactly can you help me?"

"For me to help, you are going to have to trust me," said the skunk. "First thing is to follow me through this door."

Brightman watched the skunk walk through the lighted door and vanish. "Well, are you coming?" asked a voice.

John rubbed his head and walked through the door. He felt weightlessness and the world around him change. His vision grew blurry, and then he found himself standing in a barren room with a cold blue marble floor. The skunk sat in front of him. "Follow me."

"Where am I?" asked Brightman.

"It's not where," said the skunk. "It's when."

Brightman followed the skunk through the vast room. Soon they entered an area housing tall bookshelves holding white and black books that extended limitlessly upward. "What is this?" asked Brightman.

The skunk disappeared, and a figure of a decrepit man in a white suit stood before him. "This is the hall of time."

"Uh, I don't know who you are," said Brightman, "but you aren't the skunk."

The old man laughed. "I am what I choose to appear to you as. The human mind cannot see my true form. I try to appear as something that is comforting."

"Skunk wouldn't be my first choice," said Brightman. "I'll go with it, though."

"What would you like my form to be?" asked the old man in the white suit. Then he shifted into a panda.

"Is this better?" asked the panda.

"Um, the old man was fine, but sure," said Brightman.

The panda shifted again into a sloth. "Let us not quibble. You are a curious subject, John Brightman."

"Yeah," said Brightman. "I'm kind of finding that out."

"If only you knew," said the sloth. "Look, I want to show you something."

The sloth waved his furry paw, and a window appeared in front of Brightman. "Take a look," said the sloth.

Brightman walked closer to the window and looked through. "What is this? That looks like me."

"It is or was," said the sloth. "This was your fate."

Brightman watched himself recite a poem as doctors gave him anesthetic. He proceeded to watch them operate and remove the recording device from his brain. "What do you mean, *was?*" he asked.

"Well, that is the curious part," said the sloth. "Your fate was sealed and the book was written, until something very curious unfolded. Months before this moment, something happened. Do you remember anything?"

"The only thing I remember is being in my bathroom when a white light hit me," said Brightman. "After that, everything went dark and I met Ashley. I don't remember anything about what happened before, but I have knowledge. Just nothing relating to me personally."

"Do you remember a Bear, Bird, and Fox?" asked the sloth.

Brightman paused. "In my dreams. They appeared in my dreams."

"What if I told you they weren't dreams?" said the Sloth, now shifting into a beagle.

"Then what are they?" asked Brightman.

"Did you see the woman in white?" asked the beagle.

"There was a woman," said Brightman, "a beautiful woman trapped in a floating sphere."

"That was Learyana," said the beagle. "She is an Eternal."

"Okay, you are losing me now," said Brightman.

"As a human, John," said the beagle, "you are very insignificant in the universe. You shouldn't even exist, as a matter of fact."

"Um, okay," Brightman said, laughing.

"Before life as you know it existed, Eternals ruled the void. Everything was fine until one Eternal, Denod, went insane. His love for Learyana became more than an obsession, and he committed the highest sin. He killed a fellow Eternal. From the blood of his brother, life formed in the void. Denod imprisoned his love and ruled over the life created with hatred greater than any perversion you may have witnessed. Look."

The beagle wagged his tail and another window appeared. Brightman gazed into a vast expanse of planets and stars. They floated through the void as lifeless husks. "What is this?" asked Brightman.

"That is all that is left of the life created by the blood of the Eternal. Denod tortured the life forms on each of the planets until every breath ceased. Now he wants to do the same to humans."

"Why didn't the other Eternals stop him?" asked Brightman.

"Denod is extremely powerful and sealed off his peers to enact his malice upon life. He lost his mind after Learyana betrayed him," said the beagle.

"Yeah, women can do that," snipped Brightman, thinking of Ashley briefly.

"Get rid of those thoughts," said the beagle. "Look again."

Brightman peered into another window that appeared before him. Images of Ashley appeared. They cast a glowing light within the darkness. "These are your memories," said the beagle. "At least what you have made so far."

"Wait a minute," said Brightman. "In a dream a small girl told me to get my own."

"Yes," said the beagle. "She was guiding you. Your memories will be the key to defeating Denod. You are linked to the Sub Blackness, Brightman. That is where Denod resides—his true form, anyway. As you create more memories, his world is shrinking."

"So, I am not dreaming?"

"Correct. What did you see when you found the woman in white?"

"She killed herself and exploded into light," said Brightman.

"Learyana gave her life to spread her light throughout the universe," said the beagle. "You happened to get hit with her light. Hence your connection to the Sub Blackness."

"So those voices and visions?" asked Brightman.

"Other people struck by Learyana's light," said the beagle.

"So, what am I supposed to do?"

"Continue to create memories, and you will find those that can help you defeat Denod," said the beagle. "Kill the creature that he is inhabiting, and his true form will be revealed if you can drive him out of the Sub Blackness."

"How?" asked Brightman.

"Begin to trust," said the beagle. "Forgive, fear, love, and live. Oh, and beware the poem. That poem spells doom for you ..."

As the talking beagle's last words entered Brightman's ears, he awoke in Prinn's ranch. Brightman rubbed his eyes and quickly got out of bed and went in search of Prinn and Ashley. "Prinn!" shouted Brightman. "Prinn where are you?"

"I'm over here," said Prinn, sitting in the chair by the computers. "I thought you went to sleep."

"I'm a light sleeper," said Brightman. "Look, you said the other Observers' recordings are linked to me?"

"Correct," said Prinn. "Here—look at this."

Prinn directed Brightman over to the various computers on his table. He made a few quick keyboard presses, and a series of graphs popped up on the screen. "Look at these lines," said Prinn. "The activity charts information being transferred into your recording device. Everything is fairly steady as each Observer transferred their info when they died. The only thing that I don't understand is here. See this spike?"

Brightman looked at the screen and nodded.

"That wasn't an information transfer. I don't know what it was, and that's when your memory dump happened," said Prinn.

"Memory dump?" asked Brightman.

"That's the point when you lost all the memories I gave you," said Prinn.

"Shortly after Ashley found me," said John. "Prinn?"

"Yes," he replied.

"Is there any way you can get the info from the recorder without turning me into a vegetable?"

"Possibly," said Prinn. "I can try to pull out the info electronically and then decode the video. I'm not saying it will work, but it might."

"Great," said Brightman.

"It's going to take some time to set up," said Prinn. "Maybe I can have it ready in a few hours. In the meantime, why don't you go talk to Ashley."

"I don't know if that's a good idea," said Brightman.

Prinn frowned. "It couldn't hurt. I can't have you two at odds. Just talk to her."

Brightman nodded.

"Well, what are you waiting for? I think she is out back by the pond with Annie."

"You have a pond?" asked Brightman.

113

"Just go and talk to her," said Prinn. "I have work to do."

Brightman left Prinn to his work and walked out the back entrance of the ranch. Scattered lights lit up the area, and Brightman made his way over to Ashley. She turned to look at him and started to get up.

"It's okay," said Brightman. "I want to talk to you."

Ashley reluctantly sat back down and looked straight ahead into the pine forests that surrounded the ranch. "Look," said Ashley. "I—"

Brightman stopped her midsentence and stared into her eyes. He quickly kissed her. Ashley hedged back and then embraced Brightman and returned his advance. John gently laid her on her back. "What are you doing?" asked Ashley, a smile running across her face.

"Making memories," said Brightman as he kissed her again, this time running his hand up her loose-fitting sweater.

"Woof," barked Annie.

Brightman looked off to the side. "Do you mind?"

Annie pawed her head and then walked back to the ranch. Brightman kissed Ashley again, and they began to make love in the thick green grass. Yellow flowers shined in the light, casting a subtle glow that reflected off the mirrorlike water of the small pond.

Brightman rolled off of Ashley and lay next to her. He cupped her hand in his as the two stared up into the cloudless sky. They talked through the night, caressing each other and making love three more times.

"What do you remember from the underground?" asked Brightman.

"What do you mean?" replied Ashley.

"What was it like growing up down there?"

"I don't remember much at all," said Ashley. "My mind got wiped so many times after the missions that things have gotten hazy."

"I can relate," said Brightman. "Look, right now, though. Me and you. These are our memories."

Ashley rolled onto her side. "What good is it? I can't get you back to the underground, and if I did, you know what would happen."

"There could be another way," said Brightman. "I talked to Prinn and he is working on something. He may be able to get the info we need without making me a vegetable."

Ashley turned back to Brightman. "Then what? What can we do? We have no army or people to help even if we could get the information the Elders hoped for."

"I don't believe that," said Brightman. "I think others are helping us."

"You mean the ghosts who painted the cave pictures?" snipped Ashley. "We will need more than ghosts."

Ashley rolled away from Brightman and put on her clothes. "I'm going inside for a bit."

Brightman sighed and stared up at the sky again. "Brightman!" shouted Prinn. "Brightman, get in here."

Prinn's voice jostled John from his thoughts, and he quickly put his clothes on and headed inside.

"Did you figure it out?" asked Brightman.

"I think so," said Prinn. "Did you talk to Ashley?"

"Yeah."

"How did it go?"

"Good," said Brightman. "What was so important that you had to see me right now?"

"Hmm, was I interrupting something?" asked Prinn.

"Interrupting what?" asked Ashley as she walked into the room and sat down in the barrel chair. Annie followed her and pawed at Ashley's knee. She petted Annie and smiled slightly.

"I thought you didn't like dogs," Brightman said.

"She has grown on me," said Ashley.

"Chocolate Labs can do that to people," said Prinn,

"How do you have a dog anyway?" asked Ashley.

"I grew her like I did Brightman," said Prinn. "Anyway. Listen to this."

Prinn turned up the volume on a speaker. "There was a message that was on loop for some time. I never thought anything of it because until now I had never heard this. Listen."

The three listened intently to Bird's message from the air base. Prinn played it a few times to satisfy their disbelief.

"Bird," said Brightman. "If that's the Bird from the missing recon team, she may have answers. We should find her."

"I agree that hearing another person's voice is comforting, but I wouldn't rush to anything," said Prinn.

"We are going to need help once you get the info out of my head," said Brightman.

"Ah yeah," said Prinn. "It's a shot in the dark, but I think it will work."

"Well, what are we waiting for?" asked Brightman.

Prinn turned off the speaker and ushered Brightman into the room he had given him to sleep in. "All right, lie down," said Prinn.

Brightman followed Prinn's instructions and stretched out on the small cot. Prinn attached a few wires to Brightman's temples and inserted the other end of the wires into a small hard drive. He left the room for a few minutes and then returned with a needle. "I'm just going to inject you with this. It's a mild sedative with a few other homemade ingredients to help you relax."

"All right," said Brightman.

Prinn left the room again and returned with a thick metal vest that he placed on Brightman's chest. He ran some wires on top of it. "I'm just going to stimulate you with a small electrical current. Might sting."

Ashley moved closer to Brightman and took his hand in hers. John mumbled as Prinn's concoction clouded his mind. *That's more than a sedative*, thought Brightman as he began to feel detached from his body. The electrical current began coursing through Brightman's muscles and brain. He felt his heart begin to beat faster, and a pain in his chest began to grow rapidly until Brightman drifted into unconsciousness.

"Clear!" shouted Prinn as he jolted Brightman with electricity.

Brightman's chest jolted violently upward, and his eyes burst open. He gasped for air and looked around the room. "What happened?"

"You went into cardiac arrest," said Prinn. "Sorry. I've never actually done this before."

Ashley placed a soft wool blanket on John and rubbed his arm. He smiled at her and then glared at Prinn. "Please at least say it worked," said Brightman.

"Well, I got something," said Prinn. "I'll need time to convert the files to video. Get some sleep."

Prinn left the room and looked back as Ashley sat by Brightman's side. He hid his smile and then disappeared into the ranch. "Let's go, Annie," said Prinn.

THE DOG HAS
GOGGLES ON

Brightman sat on a wicker chair in a crow's nest atop the roof of the ranch—the same one Prinn had used to spy on Ashley and John when they had stumbled upon his home. He could see the expanse of the area around him. Solar panels covered the roof of the ranch, and wires ran to a series of generators on the ground. The tall metal windmills also helped provide Prinn with the power to run his electronics and other gizmos that needed electricity. The pond in the back provided Prinn with water that he filtered as well as the supply of fish he had been giving them to eat. Bass definitely didn't taste the best, but anything tasted better than the bland paperlike ration cubes. The idea of staying here with Ashley crossed Brightman's mind, but that idea felt like a cop-out. A sense of duty filled Brightman's heart. Many people had sacrificed their lives for him to be alive. Hiding away and watching the world die didn't sit right with him. Brightman left the crow's nest and climbed down a ladder to the grass below. He noticed a bulky object covered in a green tarp to the left of the ranch. *I didn't see that before*, he thought.

Ashley tossed a white ball with Annie near the edge of the pine trees. The Lab eagerly retrieved the ball each time Ashley tossed it. Annie would run back to Ashley and mouth her hands and then drop the ball. The two kept up the game of fetch, unaware that Brightman was watching them. John walked over to the tarp, which covered something from view. John ran his hand over the weathered hemp cover, and an image entered his mind. The white lines and computer nodes he had seen in the Sub Blackness and when he had picked up Ashley's camouflage device filled his head. He closed his eyes, and pages of words and experiences flooded his mind. Brightman removed his hand from the tarp. He knew that underneath the tarp sat an old modified army chopper. Brightman understood the mechanics of how to operate it, and he thought he could fly it. He rubbed his head again and stepped back from the tarp.

"Brightman," said Prinn from behind him.

John jumped at Prinn's voice. "Yes, Prinn."

"I think I found what we are looking for," said Prinn. "Meet me inside in the computer room."

"Sure, Prinn," said Brightman. "I'll be there in a few minutes."

Brightman decided to leave Ashley playing with Annie and went to see what Prinn had discovered with the information from his head.

"You are going to want to sit down for this," said Prinn.

Brightman took a seat next to Prinn and watched him pore over the data. "Most of this is useless," said Prinn. "However, there's this bit here. I don't know how this Observer wandered where he did, but look."

Brightman watched the moments from another Observer's mind play out in front of him. The man walked over rugged terrain through a dying forest. He found the entrance to a cave and walked through a deep tunnel.

"There it is," said Prinn. "Look: that's the source."

Brightman looked at the picture on the computer screen. A large pink substance sat in the depths of a cave. Its shape seemed fluid in nature and its size limitless. The outside of the creature resembled the look of a giant brain. Large sacs littered the sides, and long tentacles extended and disappeared into the ground. Every so often a membrane would open, revealing a large yellow eye. Creatures of all shapes and sizes emerged from the sacs along the sides of the monstrosity.

"Is it giving birth?" asked Brightman.

"I'm not sure," said Prinn, "but that is definitely where the smaller creatures originate from."

"Can you get coordinates? Can we locate it?" asked Brightman.

"I think so," said Prinn.

"Then we can use the helicopter to fly to Bird," said Brightman.

"How do you know I have a helicopter?" asked Prinn. "And even if I did, nobody here can fly it."

"I can," said Brightman.

"That's impossible," said Prinn.

"Normally I would agree with you," said Brightman, "but something in my head changed when I got hit by that light—the energy spike you saw."

"What do you mean?" asked Prinn.

"I seem to be able to figure stuff out or learn things," said Brightman. "Mainly it's been with mechanical devices. I know how they work and operate. It's like information is beamed into my head."

"Interesting," said Prinn. "I'd like to run some tests."

"We don't have time," said Brightman. "I want to get moving. The faster we get to Bird, the closer we are to finding a way to stop this thing."

"Fair enough," said Prinn. "We will leave first thing in the morning. I have to pack my gear. I suggest you and Ashley do the same. I have some backpacks you can use."

"Great," said Brightman. "I'll let Ashley know."

"Wait. Brightman," said Prinn. "There is something I need to tell you."

Brightman looked at Prinn strangely. "Okay, but now isn't the best time."

Prinn reached into a drawer and produced a picture of a woman with long black hair in a white lab coat holding a newborn. He handed the picture to Brightman. John looked at the picture a moment and then looked at Prinn. "Who is that?" asked Brightman.

Prinn didn't answer at first, and then spoke softly. "That is your mother, John. Sharon Pin."

Brightman didn't speak. He looked at the picture and then at Prinn. "I thought you said you grew me."

"Sharon and I had trouble having kids at the time," said Prinn. "The Elders agreed to help Sharon give birth to you if we worked with them on the Observer project. My wife gave birth, and we kept you for a short time before the Elders took you from us."

"Why didn't you tell me this earlier?" asked Brightman, looking confused and a bit angry.

"I wasn't sure how you would react," said Prinn.

"So that would make you my father," said Brightman.

Prinn nodded. "I should have told you. I'm sorry."

"What happened to my mother?" asked Brightman, running his finger across the outline of the woman.

Prinn rubbed his eye. "After we left the surface, we wandered around for a while. We met some other people and settled with them for a while. Sharon and I grew tired of their power trips and petty squabbles, so we left. Many of the people who stayed on the surface are the same as the Elders. Always it seems someone is looking to control someone else or worse. We settled here and worked on Sharon's research."

"The plants and stuff?" asked Brightman.

"Yes," said Prinn. "Sharon expanded her research and created an accelerant that helped things grow faster. Unfortunately, she grew ill before she could perfect it."

"What happened?" asked Brightman.

"My wife got sick and a year later passed away," said Prinn. "Cancer. Something that the underground could have helped with, most likely."

Brightman handed the picture back to Prinn. "I'm sorry."

"I'm the one who should be sorry, Brightman," said Prinn.

John looked at his father's old worn face and pushed away the feelings of anger. "It's okay. We have some work ahead of us. After all this is done, we can sit down for a talk." He smiled.

Prinn put the photo in a drawer and returned to the video footage. "You should probably find Ashley," said Prinn.

Brightman nodded and went in search of Ashley. John told her about what Prinn had discovered. He left out the part about Prinn being his father. Brightman wanted to hold that for a different time, and he still felt unsure about his emotions. They spent most of the night packing gear for the trip, and the remainder of the time before sunrise in bed. The morning came quickly and interrupted the two lovers. John didn't want to get out of bed but forced himself up, slowly put clothes on, and grabbed his backpack.

"Prinn is probably waiting for us," said Brightman.

Ashley shrugged and reluctantly followed Brightman's lead. They walked outside and saw Prinn and Annie sitting near the helicopter. "Um, who is going to fly that?" asked Ashley.

"I am," said Brightman as he opened the door to the cockpit and hopped in. He effortlessly flipped a few switches and began the vehicle's prep for flight.

Prinn joined him, taking the other seat in the cockpit. Annie hopped into the back area and sat down. On her head a large pair of goggles covered her eyes. Ashley placed her backpack inside and took a seat near Annie. "The dog has goggles on?" she said, smirking. "Um, okay."

"She has sensitive eyes," said Prinn.

"Woof," barked Annie, opening her mouth wide and looking around. The base of her chin was speckled with gray hairs, giving her the appearance of having a beard.

"All right, everybody, buckle up," said Brightman.

"Are you sure you know what you're doing?" asked Ashley. "I don't recall you mentioning that you could fly."

"Relax," said Brightman. "I have many hidden talents. My last name is Brightman, after all."

Ashley rolled her eyes. "Just don't kill us."

The engines of the helicopter erupted, and its heavy blades began to spin. "We won't be able to make it in one trip," said Prinn. "The solar panels I rigged will need to recharge."

"No problem," said Brightman. "You just navigate the course and I'll do the rest."

"I'll pray we don't die," said Ashley.

"Woof," barked Annie.

NICE TO MEET YOU

The heavy treads of the jump vehicle rolled across the uneven ground of the wasteland. Occasionally a stray rock broke under the weight of the vehicle and caused a few bumps for the occupants, who rode in silence. Ed glanced back at Yanti and Lesly sitting in the rigid seats. They hadn't said much to Ed since arriving on the surface. From time to time Yanti would glance out a small round window and take in the surroundings. Ed remembered the shock he had felt upon seeing the surface on his first recon mission. The stark brutality of the world around them caused many people to grow hopeless and cagey. Although the open skies provided relief from the claustrophobic halls of the underground, the utter destruction that the world lay in could be overwhelming. Ed had received Bird's transmission a day or so earlier. He had refrained from replying for fear that the underground might be listening. He didn't want anyone following him.

The terrain didn't have many structures of notable size remotely close. Ed preferred the open wasteland. The lack of major buildings grouped together made the chances of running into any creatures fairly low. Most of the monstrosities preferred the cities or clumps of buildings for nesting purposes. Out here, in the wastes, a stray pack might pop up from time to time—nothing the jump vehicle couldn't handle.

In the first few hours of arriving on the surface, Ed let Yanti and Lesly explore the area and gave their eyes time to adjust to the sunlight, in contrast to the faux light provided in the underground. He also went over the use of the two sets of combat armor the jump vehicle stored: blue-and-white suits that allowed the user faster movement packed with quite a bit of firepower. The right arm housed a mini gun that held an unlimited capacity of ammo as long as the power supply didn't overheat from firing. The left arm held an extendable blade for combat in close quarters, and a flame unit. The armor didn't take much practice, but Ed wanted his companions to get acquainted with the weaponry in case they needed it. The back of the jump vehicle contained a large turret that extended upon command controlled in the cockpit area. The turret provided quite a punch but took time to recharge after every shot.

The sun began to dip slightly in the sky, and daylight shrank. On the horizon Ed spotted a structure and decided to stop the vehicle. "Why did we stop?" asked Lesly, breaking the silence.

Ed left the cockpit, grabbed some binoculars, and exited the vehicle. "There is something in the distance. I want to take a look at it before we roll on up," he said as he stepped outside.

He raised the binoculars to his eyes and adjusted the zoom. A two-story building with broken-down walls appeared, cutting through the endless line of the horizon. The structure extended quite a bit outward, and a lone tower sat atop the right side. A large antenna stretched to the sky from atop the tower. Ed couldn't see any movement within the structure. "There is definitely something up ahead," said Ed. "What do you guys think?"

"Beats driving in this tank endlessly," said Yanti.

"I agree," said Lesly "I think we should give it a look."

Ed spent a few more minutes looking over the landscape and entered the vehicle. "Alright," he said. "Just keep your eyes peeled for trouble."

The tank rolled forward again, breaking rocks and turning them into dust. They had traveled for another hour when a shot ricocheted off the cockpit. The bullet just grazed the protective glass, serving as a warning shot. "Looks like we've got company," said Ed, stopping the tank. "You two stay inside. If anything happens, shut the door and get out of here."

"What about you?" asked Lesly.

Ed didn't reply and cautiously exited the vehicle. He moved slowly and stepped in front of the tank with his arms in the air. In the distance he could make out the form of a man atop the roof of the structure, holding a rifle. In the sky a figure soared toward him. It seemed human with arms outstretched, almost as if it were surfing the breeze. Ed could see the figure clearly now. The slight form of a woman descended toward

Ed. She lowered her arms and softly skidded across the red dust-covered ground to stand in front of him. The woman was adorned in a light blue jumpsuit with a baby fastened to her chest in a makeshift carrier, and wore a blue-jay-like mask. He immediately recognized the gear as recon. Not just any recon: that type of jumpsuit went only to the elite of the elite.

"You must be Bird," said Ed, keeping his arms in the air and standing still. He spoke softly and maintained eye contact with the woman in front of him. "And the little one?"

The woman withdrew a katana from her back and held it near her side. "How do you know my name?" asked Bird. "Keep in mind a rifle is aimed at your head. His name is Leaf, and he is my child."

"You do know that given the direction that guy is aiming, he is more likely to hit you than me," said Ed. "I'm from the underground. I left with my friends. We heard your message."

"Stand down, Jessup," said Bird into her COMM.

"Are you sure?" asked Jessup. "I can take him out if you need me to."

"It's all right," said Bird as she lowered her katana. "You don't look like any recon agent I've ever seen. You look more like a street hustler from the common than anything."

"I could say the same about you," said Ed. "That recon suit isn't standard issue, and I've never seen a recon agent with a baby. My name is Ed, and I'm looking for someone. I have two friends in the vehicle. They had to come with me to the surface. There is a bit of a problem down below."

"Let me see them," said Bird.

"Hey guys," said Ed. "It's okay. Come out here."

Yanti and Lesly slowly stepped out of the vehicle and waved to Bird. "Is that a baby?" asked Lesly.

Bird motioned to Jessup, and he left his position on the roof. "Well," said Bird. "I'll show you the way in the air base. You can park your tank, and Jessup and I will set up your quarters. We have food if you are hungry. Once you are all settled, we can talk more."

Ed lowered his hands and smiled. "That's great. Do you need a lift? We have room inside."

"No," said Bird. She dug her feet into the ground, bolted ahead, and jumped into the air. She stretched out her arms, and webbing extended from her waist to the forearms of the jumpsuit. The soft breeze that haunted the area lifted her into the sky, and she soared toward the air base.

"Wow," said Yanti.

"Does anyone find it odd that she has a baby strapped to her chest?" asked Lesly.

"I have never seen the elite recon agents. The information you hacked from the Elders database must be true. That is Bird from the missing recon team. As for the little one, that's unusual for a recon agent in the field."

Ed motioned to his friends to head back into the vehicle. He took a seat in the cockpit and got the tank rolling toward the air base. The sun began to dip faster behind the mountainous areas to the west, and the light grew scant. Ed navigated the tank through an opening in the wall and noticed Bird standing on the roof of the structure. She motioned to the right. Ed turned the tank and drove around the structure toward a hangar. He parked the tank inside and grabbed his gear. He issued quick commands to his companions, who followed suit, and the trio exited the tank. A diminutive man with a crop of messy red hair ran up to greet Ed and his friends. A long rifle banged against his shoulder secured by a longer strap.

"Hi, my name is Jessup. Nice to meet you."

IT BEGINS

The Speaker sat in a burnt-out room of a forgotten building in the common, far away from the Elders' ears and eyes. Candles lined the walls and the back of an old moldy desk in the center of the room. A man entered through the lone doorway and stood in front of the Speaker. He knelt down and spoke. "Everything is ready. We are just waiting for your command."

The Speaker didn't look at the man. He stared down with his hands folded, preparing for his journey. After a few moments he looked up and smiled. "It is time. It is time to call back all the favors and time for those in debt to repay. Carry out the plan as intended. Your sacrifice begins a new era. We will meet again in the Sub Blackness. We will all live again."

The man nodded. "Very well. Will you be coming with us?"

"No," said the Speaker. "I have important matters to attend to."

"With him?" asked the man. "The Black Mist?"

"I do his bidding as you do," said the Speaker. "Now go. Fulfill what is owed and carry out his wishes."

"I understand," said the man. He paused once to look at the Speaker again. Then he left the abandoned house.

The Speaker watched the man leave and then began to clear his mind. He let his thoughts bleed away into the Sub Blackness. The air in the building grew cold, and the candles fluttered as Black Mist began to swirl in front of the speaker. The mist held no form and encircled the body of the Speaker.

"Is everything ready?" asked a voice. "Are my followers holding up their end of the bargain?"

"Yes," said the Speaker. "And our agreement?"

The Black Mist moved more quickly around the Speaker. "Very well."

The Speaker lowered his head as the mist engulfed him. The area around him began to fade from view, and a sensation of flying overtook his body. He moved quickly and watched the world around him blur. The Black Mist shrouded his body like a cocoon as it carried him through the sky. Blackness overtook his eyes and then began to fade as the night sky of the surface appeared before his eyes. He moved quickly among the clouds, and time began to lose relevance. The Speaker noticed that he was starting to descend to the ground below. A campfire with five men became visible. The Black Mist slowed and rested on the ground near the campfire. It swirled wildly, kicking up red dust and bits of debris. The Speaker felt control over his body return, and he walked out of the mist into view. The five men nearby knelt in front of him. "He is here," said one of the men.

The mist faded into the night, and the Speaker stood in front of his followers. "My brothers," said the Speaker, "it is time. Our enemies stir in the east."

"Our brothers are on their way from the west as I speak," said one of the men. "Look."

He motioned with his arm to garner the Speaker's attention and pointed to the distance. Light trails of rocket engines from jump ships became visible—a few at first, and then more and more until the sky lit up with the fire from the flame trails of the vehicles. "Our brothers are on their way," said one of the men. "A day's travel at best."

"Good," said the Speaker. "We will need to move toward the east."

"There is a settlement not far away. They have weapons and supplies," said one of the men.

"Good," said the Speaker again. "We will invite them to join our brotherhood. If they refuse, they will meet another fate."

The Speaker raised his arms and looked toward the heavens. The light of the fire was reflected in his cold eyes. "Soon," he said, "soon this war will be done, and we shall retake our place led by the Black Mist."

The men bowed and said in unison, "Follow the Speaker to life eternal. Through the Sub Blackness we will be unified and as one. Hail the Black Mist."

* * * *

The members of the riot squad that remained barricaded themselves in the headquarters. Blast shields covered the doors and windows: standard protocol during a massive breach. Squad members lay bleeding in the streets, and the Speaker's followers rounded up whoever resisted. The mob of people moved quickly and overwhelmed the riot squad. A few escaped and disappeared into the dark maze of the common.

A short man sat in an office in front of a COMM unit. He began to record a message: "This is Eastern Base 502. We have lost control of everything. The people from the common revolted and took over all facilities. These people aren't normal. They scream and rant about the Sub Blackness as they run through the streets. Some of the riot squad joined them. They didn't have much of a choice. Either join or meet your fate with the damned. Those in my squad retreated to the barracks, but it's only a matter of time before the mob breaks through. They have forced the Elders into a safe room. The mob has assembled a large group of people to watch the Elders' area. No one of is getting in or out as far as anyone can tell. A while ago the mob destroyed the red-light stealth unit of the base. To make matters worse, rumors are floating around about a Rig sighting a few days ago. If that thing notices the base, we are all dead. I'm not sure if anyone made it out on a jump ship. Things are bad down here. No responses from the Pacific base at all anymore. The remaining men are getting antsy and are planning to try to reach the jump ships. I am putting this message on loop for anyone left out there. These could be our last days."

* * * *

The twelve Elders gathered around a large stone table. None of them knew for sure how long they had been in the room. They had nowhere to go. An angry mob assembled in front of the lone door and stood guard. If any of the Elders decided to leave, the mob would cut them down. The lights high above the Elders on the metal ceiling flickered before going dark.

"Is that it?" asked an Elder. "Did we lose power?"

"Not sure," said another.

The Elders moved to the center of the room and huddled around each other. A faint chanting began to fill the room. The mob in front of the large doors dropped to their knees, and a hymn sounded from their souls.

"What are they doing?" asked one of the Elders.

"I don't know," replied another.

The safe room began to shake, and a large crash sent the sound of cutting metal into the Elders' eardrums. Another loud thud was followed by a larger crash. The ceiling of the room began to split open. A large yellow eye peered through the hole and then disappeared. Two large claws forced their way through the metal and spread the hole apart. An enormous head poked through. Two yellow eyes peered at the twelve Elders huddled in a circle. The creature's skin dripped with fluid from the tank. Its black flesh appeared as dark as the shadows. It opened its large maw to reveal massive teeth the size of a man's body. From within the mouth a large black tongue rolled out and dangled over the Elders. Smaller black tongues sprouted from the larger mass that hovered over their heads. These smaller tongues searched out the Elders and ran their slime-covered caress over the hapless prey's wincing flesh.

The creature's large claws forced the hole open even more, and its head stretched through the opening, hovering inches above the men. It opened its mouth wide and crashed into the group, devouring the men in one chomp. Pink fluid from the tank rolled into the room, and the creature withdrew from the hole it had entered in a flash. The mob outside the door continued to chant.

PLANTING THE SEEDS
OF REVENGE

Marybeth ran through the darkness of the wasteland, covered in the blood of her companions. The creatures struck in the dark of the night. She had escaped as her friends offered morsels for the creatures to feast upon. Behind her she could hear the screams of the helpless victims and the sound of ripping flesh. She ran across the barren landscape, breathing heavily and clutching a large combat knife tightly in her right hand. A small rusted-out camper came into view, and Marybeth jumped inside, closing the door and pushing a moldy chair in front of it. She crawled onto a rotting bed and sat against the wall of the camper, wrapping her arms around her knees. Blood ran down her forehead, and fear filled her bones. A loud thud rattled into her ears as something landed on the roof of the rusted camper. Marybeth remained silent as scratching noises ran across the top of her shelter. A small hole above her allowed the little bit of moonlight to creep through. A clear, sticky fluid began to drip from above, and a large tube like appendage lowered into the camper.

"Fuck," whispered Marybeth, her body growing tense.

The appendage extended farther and began to feel around the area. The end of the tube opened to reveal tiny razor-sharp teeth. Marybeth quickly grabbed the appendage with her left hand and cut it in half with her combat knife. The creature on the roof of the camper screamed in pain and banged and scratched the roof. A large clawed hand covered in reddish-yellow skin poked through the hole and swung about. Marybeth slashed at it with her knife, cutting deep into its flesh. The creature screamed again and withdrew its hand. Marybeth could hear the creature move about on top of the camper. Another guttural scream was followed by silence.

Marybeth kicked the severed appendage into the corner and peered through the hole. The dark night sky stared back at her, and no sign of the creature amidst the light of the moon found her sight. Marybeth crawled back into the rotting bed and curled up, holding her knees with her left arm. Her eyes darted around the camper, and she stayed vigilant through the night until sleep gained control over her body.

Marybeth awoke in a daze and swung her knife around. The night sky had been replaced by warm sunshine. She moved the old chair away from the door and stumbled out of the camper. Marybeth walked back toward her encampment and found the remains of her companions. She knelt down by one of the bodies and began laughing. She stared at the corpse for a moment and then began cutting into its flesh with her knife. Blood escaped the wound and ran across the ground. Marybeth stuffed her hands into the cut and pulled out muscle and flesh. She laughed again and again, wiping the blood and bits of flesh across her face. Her laughter began to turn manic as she covered her body with the man's innards. Marybeth started to cry, and she lay on her back, staring up at the scattered clouds. The blood from the man began to harden on her skin as the sun beat down. Marybeth drifted away, her mind racing and emotions running into the recesses of her soul. She turned to her side and clutched the combat knife tightly. It was then that a shadow broke the rays of sunlight and Marybeth turned to look at a man standing above her.

"My child," said the man's voice. "You look lost."

"Who are you?" asked Marybeth.

"I am someone who can help," said the man.

"Why would I want your help?"

"You want the Bird dead?" asked the man.

"How do you know that?" asked Marybeth.

"I also want the Bird dead," said the man. "My reasons may be different from yours, but we share the same goals."

"Here, let me help you up," said the man. "My followers call me the Speaker. My name is Ebene."

MEETING THE
OBSERVER

The old army chopper made its way across the clouds. The surface raced by until the structure of the air base became visible. Brightman pointed to the building, and Prinn nodded. The helicopter slowed and then began to circle the air base. A lone woman stood on the rooftop, and she waved at the chopper. Moments later, a few other people appeared on the roof and gathered around her. Brightman made another pass over the air base and then slowly lowered the vehicle near a hangar. The chopper hovered a minute and then plopped to the ground, jostling those inside. Red dust kicked up into the air and then settled as the spinning blades came to a stop.

Brightman and his friends grabbed their gear and slowly exited the helicopter. The people on the roof walked over to its edge and stared down upon the group. "Is this the place?" asked Brightman.

"According to my coordinates it should be," said Prinn, petting Annie as she walked over to his side.

"Ed!" exclaimed Ashley. "Ed, is that you?"

"Sure as I shit two times every Tuesday!" shouted Ed from the rooftop.

Ed slid down a ladder and ran over to Ashley. "I can't believe it!" he yelled. "Ashley."

Ashley put down her backpack and hugged Ed. Brightman stepped back and watched the two embrace. "You two know each other?" he asked.

Ashley stepped back from Ed. "Oh, where are my manners," she said. "Ed, this is John Brightman, Prinn Pin, and Annie."

Ed looked at the ragtag group quizzically. "John Brightman as in the Observer, the last Observer?"

"That's what they tell me," said Brightman.

Ed motioned to his companions on the roof and they joined him. "This is Bird, Jessup, and Leaf."

"Bird," said Brightman. "The voice on the transmission we heard."

Bird stood in silence, moving the scarlet cover over Leaf's eyes to shield him from the bright sunlight. Leaf whimpered and then grew silent, his tiny hands clinging to a strap from the makeshift carrier. "My partner Bear was looking for you," said Bird. "He was tasked to find Observers."

Brightman remembered his visions and the paintings in the cave. "You have a friend called Fox?" he asked.

Bird paused again. "Fox and Bear are dead."

Annie gently walked over to Bird and sniffed Leaf before sitting down. Bird stepped back and grew tense. "She won't hurt you," said Prinn. "Her name is Annie."

Bird relaxed a bit. "You know Ed. This is Lesly and Yanti." Yanti and Lesly slowly gathered around Bird, looking at the newcomers to the air base.

Bird's companions said their hellos and stood quietly by her side. She slowly removed the blue-jay-like helmet from her head. Long blond hair fell around her shoulders, and her blue eyes glistened in the sunlight.

"We have come here in search of help," said Brightman. "We have found the location of the origin point of the creatures."

"The biggie," said Ed. "You know where the biggie is?"

Brightman nodded. "We can't reach the creature alone. Do you still have contact with the underground?"

"We are all that's left," said Ed. "We received a transmission—"

"What are you saying?" asked Ashley.

"They are gone, Ashley," said Ed.

"The only thing we have here are a few weapons and an old jump tank," said Jessup.

"What about that?" asked Prinn, pointing to the decrepit jet in the hangar.

"Good luck with that," said Yanti. "If we can even repair it, no one here can fly the damn thing."

"I can," said Brightman. "Well, I should be able to, anyway."

"Why don't we go inside," said Prinn. "I can explain more."

The group nodded in approval, and Bird's companions helped the surprise guests carry their gear into the air base. Jessup placed their packs in spare rooms. Prinn motioned for Jessup to leave his backpack alone and then gathered the group around a large table. He took a large wrinkled map out of the inside pocket and laid it across the table. "Look," said Prinn. "This is where we are now."

Prinn's finger centered on the air base. The map, an older representation of the United States, showed the location to be in Kansas. He moved his finger upward to South Dakota. "This is where the creature is. If we can get that jet up and running, Brightman can fly it and deliver a strike to the creature. Ideally he'll be able to destroy it."

"That's everything we've been fighting for in recon," said Ed.

"It's what we've all been fighting for," said Prinn.

"I can get to work on fixing the jet," said Yanti. "I might be able to use some parts from the jump vehicle."

"I can help," said Brightman.

"I usually work alone," said Yanti.

"Trust me, I have a knack for this sort of thing," said Brightman.

"All right, then, let's get to work," said Prinn.

* * * *

While Brightman and Yanti struggled with the repairs on the jet fighter, Prinn and Annie walked around the perimeter of the base. Prinn noticed the growth of grass that had extended from the air base. He took a few clippings and placed them in a specimen jar. Annie sniffed the grass and then wagged her tail.

"What do you think, Annie?" asked Prinn.

"Woof," barked Annie.

Prinn walked around the base a bit more and then returned to his room inside. He set up a makeshift lab with the area Jessup provided for him. He immediately placed the grass clippings on a glass slide and looked at them under a microscope. The clippings looked fairly

135

normal, save for a strange white glow that surrounded bits of the grass blades. Bird entered the room with Leaf and spoke to Prinn. "Jessup has prepared some dinner."

Prinn continued to stare at the grass clippings and noticed that the white light was growing brighter. He looked up and gave Bird a good once-over. "Would you come over here for a moment?"

Bird walked over to Prinn, holding Leaf tightly against her bosom. Prinn noticed that the glow became stronger as Bird and her baby stood near Prinn. "I need to check something," said Prinn. "May I hold your child for a moment."

Bird hesitated and then handed Leaf to Prinn. "Don't worry," said Prinn. "Now I need you to back away, please."

"I don't understand," said Bird.

"I'm not sure I do either, but please back away," said Prinn.

Bird slowly backed away and watched Prinn bounce Leaf on his knee. Leaf giggled, and Prinn smiled. "I don't believe what I'm seeing."

"What is it?" asked Bird.

"Here, have a look," said Prinn as he beckoned Bird over to look at the grass clippings.

Bird peered into the microscope and looked at the grass clippings shrouded in a bright white light. Leaf giggled and reached his tiny hand toward the microscope. The glass slide began to vibrate. Then bits of the grass expanded, cracking the glass slide. The growth extended across the table and down one of its legs. Bird backed away along with Prinn. Leaf giggled and moved his tiny hand to touch the green growth that spread across the table. Prinn handed Leaf back to Bird. "Would you get Lesly?" said Prinn. "I am going to need to take a sample of Leaf's blood. Tell her to bring her medical bag."

Bird cast a protective glance toward Leaf. The prospect of him sticking her child with a needle did not sit well. "It will be all right," said Prinn. "I just need a small sample. He will be fine."

Bird reluctantly left the room and returned with Lesly. Prinn instructed Lesly on the specifics. She gently took Leaf from Bird's arms and placed him on the large table. Leaf giggled and looked at Lesly, waving his arms. She carefully held one of his arms down and gently inserted a small needle. Leaf cried out and then began sobbing. "It's okay, little one," said Lesly. "Almost done."

Lesly extracted a small sample of Leaf's blood and then handed him back to Bird. He continued to cry, and Bird swayed him in her arms until his crying lessened and stopped. Prinn took the blood sample from Lesly and walked over to his pack, from which he took various pieces of equipment. "I'll be passing on dinner," said Prinn. "I need to check something out. The grass that is growing around the base: when did that start?"

"Sometime after we got here," said Bird. "Jessup noticed it."

"I'll need some privacy for a bit," said Prinn.

"Am I done here?" asked Lesly.

Prinn nodded and returned to his work. Lesly and Bird Left Prinn to his devices. Leaf began crying again, and Bird bounced him in her arms as she exited the room. "Now what do we have going on here?" mumbled Prinn.

* * * *

Jessup placed the dinner he had prepared on the table for his guests. He had scraped together bits and pieces from the supplies he found to craft a fairly tasteless dinner. Those present to eat did so in silence. Yanti and Brightman continued to work on the jet through the night while Prinn stayed in his lab. Ed related what he knew to Ashley and described the unrest in the underground as best he could. Bird didn't say much about her friends Bear and Fox. Ed tried to pry a bit, but she avoided giving away much information. "I suggest we set up a watch," said Ed. "When I was in the underground, I heard that this Sub Blackness cult seems to think Brightman is responsible for all this. They believe in some sort of Black Mist as their god."

"The Black Mist is real," said Bird. "I've seen it."

Ed perked up and looked at Bird. "What exactly happened with your recon group?"

Bird hesitated a moment. Then the radio that Jessup had placed in the corner of the room began to play a soft melodic tune. "Is that music?" asked Ed.

"Yeah," said Jessup. "The radio does that."

"Strange," said Ed.

"My friends Bear and Fox encountered the Black Mist," said Bird. "It possessed Fox. We fought against it and drove it away. Fox chased after it, and that was the last I saw of her."

Ed listened as Bird recounted her tale as best she could. Her voice carried a pain within her words. She finished telling about her encounter with the Black Mist and then left the room with Leaf. Jessup got up to follow, but Lesly stopped him. He sat back down and gave a last look toward Bird as she disappeared into the base.

Brightman entered the room covered in grease and oil. "I think we are done," he said.

"Where is Yanti?' asked Ed.

"He mentioned something about boosting the signal on the radio transmitter," said Brightman. "I'm starving. Is there any food left?"

"I'll fix a plate," said Jessup.

Brightman sat down next to Ashley and rubbed her thigh. She smiled at him. "We should get some rest."

"I haven't eaten yet," said Brightman.

Ashley took his hand and moved with him down the hall. "You can eat later."

Ed cast a glance toward Lesly and smiled. "You know, Lesly. It's been a while."

Lesly smiled at Ed and walked over to him. She kissed him gently and motioned to him to follow her. Jessup entered the room holding a plate of food. "Where did everybody go?"

"Woof," barked Annie as she sat next to Jessup.

"Oh, you," said Jessup. "Well, here you go. Enjoy."

Jessup set the plate of food on the floor, and Annie eagerly devoured the meal. Her tail wagged furiously. Then she pawed at Jessup. "Woof."

"That's all I've got," said Jessup as he petted Annie gently. Jessup shrugged and decided to retire for the night. He walked past Bird's room and paused, peeking in through the half-open door. He watched as Bird held Leaf, sobbing on her cot. Jessup lingered a bit longer before making his way to his quarters. He rolled onto his bed and stared at the ceiling. Annie walked into the room, pawed at Jessup, and then sat down on the floor and huffed. Jessup decided to scroll some thoughts on a piece of paper. His mind drifted to Bird, and his feelings for her began to stir.

* * * *

Ed rolled off of Lesly, sweat dripping from his face. He smiled and kissed her, and then got up and dressed. "That was quick," said Lesly. "Like always."

"Sorry, baby," said Ed. "I want to check out the area a bit. I have a feeling we have unwanted guests, and I want to be prepared."

"Typical," sighed Lesly. "Hurry back."

Ed kissed Lesly once more before leaving the room. He grabbed a pair of binoculars and headed to the roof. Ed scanned the horizon. The scattered clouds that floated across the sky allowed bits of light from the moon to shine on the barren wasteland. Alone with his thoughts, Ed looked into the distance. The words of the Speaker penetrated his thoughts. He stayed on the roof for a few hours, diligently scanning the distance for any signs of life. Ed felt satisfied and decided to return to Lesly. Then he saw plumes of smoke rising in the distance. He changed the magnification on the binoculars and focused on the smoke. Shadowy figures became visible around a burning fire. Ed couldn't make out how many there were or what he was seeing, but something stirred in the distance.

PRINN'S PLAN

Prinn sat with his allies and waited until the shuffling and excess talking stopped. "Is the jet ready?" he asked.

"As far as I can tell, it will fly," said Yanti. "I'm not so sure about the bombs on the thing. I did as you instructed and rigged the big bomb with a tachyon device and installed your gizmo. What is that thing, anyway?"

"It's something that should destroy the cells of the creature," said Prinn. "Blowing it up won't do any good. Every single cell of that abomination must die. With the help of some of my wife's old research that I reverse engineered, and my secret ingredient, I think it will work."

"Yanti," said Prinn. "I am going to need you to rig the last tachyon pulse onto the jet. Brightman is going to need to use it to escape the blast."

"Fine," said Yanti. "I'll get to work on it."

Ashley removed her tachyon device and handed it to Yanti. "We are lucky. There is one charge left, courtesy of Prinn's solar panels. That will leave us without any tachyon pulses. Bird's is on the bomb and now mine for the jet."

"That's fine," said Prinn. "After this we shouldn't need them anymore."

"We have some trouble," said Ed. "Last night I noticed some activity to the west. I'm not sure what, exactly, but we could have some guests sooner rather than later."

Yanti exited the room, speaking quickly as he left. "I'll have the jet rigged in a jiffy."

"Great," said Prinn.

A few hours passed and Yanti returned to his companions. "The tachyon pulse is rigged and ready to go."

"All right," said Prinn. "Brightman, are you ready?"

"As ready as I'll ever be," said Brightman.

"Time to go," said Prinn as he left the room and headed to the hangar.

Brightman gathered the bits and pieces of an old flight suit and helmet and followed Prinn. Ashley stopped him and put her arms around his neck. Brightman looked into her soft eyes and smiled. He gently kissed her pouty lips. "Be careful," said Ashley.

"I'll be back before you know it," said Brightman. He wanted to stay in Ashley's arms, but he had more important matters at hand. Brightman placed his helmet under his arm and headed toward the hangar. Yanti greeted him at the jet and went over the tachyon pulse he had rigged for Brightman's escape. John nodded and climbed into the cockpit of the jet. Ed taxied the plane out of the hangar, using the tank, and then drove the jump vehicle to the western side of the air base. Bird stood atop the roof holding Leaf with Jessup and Prinn. Ashley looked at the jet from a distance with Lesly and Annie. She watched as the old jet began to rise into the air. The sound of the engines cut through the silence of the wasteland. The jet rose higher. Then the engines shifted, and the plane exploded into the distance, leaving a vapor trail in its wake. "It's holding together so far," said Brightman through a COMM.

"Good to hear," said Prinn. "I've put the coordinates into your flight computer. That should lead you to the creature. Once you are ready, fire the bomb. It should self-guide itself home. Once it hits, use the tachyon pulse and get out of there. The blast will melt you if you are still in range."

"Gotcha," said Brightman.

Bird watched the jet disappear into the sky. She wondered what it would be like after Brightman destroyed the creature. Leaf's small hand reached to the sky, and he giggled. Jessup turned away and walked to the back end of the roof. He kept his head down and peered at the note he had scribbled the night before. He had decided to tell Bird how he felt about her. Jessup paced the rooftop, building up the courage to confess his feelings to Bird. He had started to walk toward her when he noticed a woman covered in blood quickly climb up a ladder and head in Bird's direction, a knife drawn. Jessup screamed and ran toward the woman. He jumped and crashed into her, falling to the ground in a heap, fighting with the assailant.

Marybeth sat atop Jessup, her face covered in dried blood and her eyes reflecting madness. She raised the large combat knife and buried it deep within Jessup's chest. The blade penetrated Jessup's flesh quickly, and he screamed in pain. Bird turned to look at Jessup and yelled out in anger. She extended her arms, and light blue webbing flashed, gripping the breeze. Sunlight reflected off of Bird's helmet. She descended upon Marybeth and knocked her from atop Jessup's body. Marybeth whirled around and flashed her knife wildly. Bird drew her katana and jumped at Marybeth. The blade struck her in the leg, pinning her against the wall of the air base. Marybeth screamed in pain, trying to pull the cold steel from her thigh, but it held her fast, its blade embedded in the concrete of the air-base wall.

Bird quickly knelt by Jessup's head and held him still. Blood trickled out of his mouth, and he began to speak. "Bird, B-B-ird, B—"

"Jessup," cried Bird. "Jessup. Someone help us. Please!"

Jessup tried to speak, but blood clogged his throat as his eyes looked at Bird. "It's okay, Jessup. I'm here," said Bird.

Bird placed two hands on either side of Jessup's head and tried to ease his suffering. "B-ird," mumbled Jessup. "I- I—"

"I know, Jessup," cried Bird.

Jessup gurgled his last breath, and his dead eyes stared into the sky. Bird rose from Jessup's side and walked over to Marybeth. She pulled her katana from the woman's leg, raised her fist high in the air, and struck Marybeth in the face, sending a tooth flying from her mouth. The woman fell to the ground and didn't move. Bird raised her katana.

"No," screamed Prinn. "Be smart, Bird."

Bird looked at Prinn and then at the motionless woman, and knelt down. "Get her out of my sight!" yelled Bird.

Prinn scampered down from the roof and called for help. Ashley and Lesly made it over and took the woman into the air base. "Tie her up," said Prinn. "Maybe we can find out something from her."

Bird turned to look over Jessup's corpse. "Help me get him inside," said Bird.

* * * *

Ashley and Ed spent the next hour interrogating Marybeth. She laughed as they threatened her with violence. Her eyes darted around the room, betraying madness, and she continued to berate her inquisitors with nonsensical laughter. "This lady is batshit crazy," said Ed.

"Yeah," said Ashley, "but I don't think she came here alone."

"Guys," said Lesly through her COMM.

"What is it?" asked Ed.

"You better get up on the roof," said Lesly. "Now."

Ed and Ashley left the woman tied up and locked the door to the room. They scrambled up onto the roof and met Lesly, Yanti, and Prinn. "Where's Bird?" asked Ed.

"She's in the air base somewhere," said Lesly. "She needed some time alone."

"We have a problem," muttered Lesly as she handed the binoculars to Ed.

Ed looked into the distance and saw the army assembled before them. Hundreds, maybe thousands, of people were approaching from the west, carrying assorted weapons and wearing makeshift armor. "Shit," said Ed.

"Who are they?" asked Lesly.

"I think it's the Sub Blackness cult," said Ed.

"We can't stop that many," remarked Ashley.

"Maybe we can," said Ed. "Lesly, remember the armor in the jump vehicle?"

"Are you thinking what I'm thinking?" asked Lesly.

Ed nodded. "Ashley, find Prinn and get some rifles. You two cover us from the roofs and stay out of the line of fire. Lesly, come with me. You remember how to use that armor?"

"Sure do," said Lesly.

"Yanti," said Ed through his COMM.

"Yeah," said Yanti.

"Meet me at the tank," said Ed. "Now."

Ed and Lesly quickly made their way over to the tank and entered the armor stored in the vehicle. The helmets bore the resemblance of a lion, and the blue-and-white metal shined in the sunlight. The two moved away from the tank and set up positions in front of the approaching horde. "Yanti," said Ed. "I need you to provide some covering fire with the turret. You remember?"

"No problem," said Yanti as he jumped into the cockpit of the tank. He flicked a few switches, and a large turret extended from the backside of the tank. Struts shot out on both sides of the vehicle to lock the tank in place from the force of the turret blast.

"I need you to fire a few shots into the crowd," said Ed.

"Gotcha," said Yanti. He looked at the aiming reticule in front of him and centered the crosshairs in the middle of the approaching attackers. He paused a moment and then fired. The tank shook violently as a bright blue blast launched from the turret. It flashed through the air before striking the target. A large explosion lit up the distance, and bodies flew into the sky in bits and pieces. The approaching groups scattered.

"Now!" shouted Ed as he opened fire on the crowd. "Don't let the guns overheat."

Lesly followed suit and began firing into the attackers. The guns from the armor cut down the enemies, who began to scatter. Ashley and Prinn fired from atop the roof, picking off stray cultists. Once in a while, a shot would strike the roof of the air base, but nothing came close to them. Ed moved forward, switching between the mini gun and the flame unit. He cut through the waves of cultists, but they continued to press forward, driven by a madness devoid of care for life or fear.

"Any word on Brightman?" asked Ed. "I don't know how much longer we can hold them off."

Yanti sent another blast from the turret into the sea of cultists. Again, the blast ripped apart their bodies and caused blood to rain down onto those who had escaped the blast. "Don't worry, Ed," said Yanti. "I've got your back."

"Brightman," said Prinn. "Brightman, are you there?"

The COMM remained silent. "He's not responding," said Prinn.
"Then it's just us for now," screamed Ed.

* * * *

Brightman navigated the skies and entered the target area. He noticed the entrance of the cave from the video he had watched of the Observer. Creatures walked the ground, some attacking others in the midst of the dead surface. The area near the cave showed no signs of natural life. Various mutations of plant life covered the land for miles around. Their unnatural vines and growths undulated in the sunlight that beat down upon the ground. The targeting computer clicked on, and Brightman could see his quarry light up on his screen. He waited until the crosshairs turned green and then unloaded the payload. The bomb fell from the jet and made its way toward the heart of the creature. The guidance system directed it through the long cavern to its destination.

Brightman pulled up and turned the jet away. A strange white electrical aura emanated from the ground, and then waves of purple washed over the horizon. Brightman clicked the tachyon pulse Yanti had rigged, and the jet disappeared in a blink. The purple waves that extended from the bomb withdrew into the center. A large white explosion shot forth, sending shock waves into the air. The ground rumbled, and then heavy green grass began to expand from the explosion, covering the surface as it spread rapidly across the land.

Brightman's jet exited the tachyon pulse, and the air base appeared in view. Behind Brightman the grass grew faster, creating large vines and trees that sprouted up as well as flowers of all colors. Brightman watched as a sea of yellow, blue, red, orange, purple, and green covered the once barren and destroyed land. "Uh, Prinn," said Brightman, "what did you put in that bomb?"

Brightman's voice popped in Prinn's COMM. "Brightman!"

"It's me, Prinn," said Brightman. "I dropped the bomb, but uh ..."

Prinn looked into the distance and saw the jet approaching. He noticed the sea of growth expanding upon the land. "I may have used too much accelerant."

"Shit," said Brightman. "The jet is breaking apart!"

Brightman kept hold of the flight stick as pieces of the jet began to break off around him. He soared over the air base and began to descend toward the ground, which was now a sea of flowers, grass, vines, and trees. He made sure the jet cleared the air base before ejecting as the vehicle crashed, creating a small ball of flame. He floated to the ground and landed in a field of multicolored flowers. Ashley noticed the parachute open and left the roof and headed toward Brightman.

Ed continued his assault on the cultists as large vines grew around him, ultimately wrapping around the armor and preventing him from moving. He looked into the distance and noticed the man from the underground at the riot Ed had suppressed. The man squirmed as vines wrapped around his arms and legs, holding him fast. His followers ran in disarray, trying to escape the sea of growth sprouting up in all directions.

Brightman was lying on his back fumbling with the parachute when Ashley came into view and knelt by his side. He smiled, but then pain shot through his body. He couldn't move, and his vision began to blur. Ashley reached out to him, and pain coursed through her body. The world around Brightman and Ashley grew dark.

Lights began to flash, and Brightman recognized the Sub Blackness. He looked to his side and saw Ashley standing next to him. An ethereal mist darted in front of him. It made a quick move to a crack in the light. Brightman grabbed Ashley, and light shot forth from his hand, covering the darkness with a stained-glass-like burst of energy of a memory. The Black Mist shrieked and ran toward another bit of darkness.

"Ashley," screamed Brightman. "Use your memories. Our memories can trap the creature."

Brightman stood with his back against Ashley's, and the two emitted their memories in beams of white light, cutting off the retreat of the Black Mist and filling the Sub Blackness with cascading streams of light and moving pictures. "We need more memories," said Brightman. "Ashley, I need you to remember."

Ashley continued to throw beams of light toward the darkness. Strange visions began to appear in the residues of the shadows. She took out the small yarn stick figure she had found in the cave. Images of

Ashley's father appeared. "Father, no!" screamed Ashley as she collapsed to the ground.

Brightman looked at the images forming. A small girl hid in the darkness as a man followed her. He held a belt and slammed it against the ground. The girl cried and held tightly to a small yarn stick figure as the man approached. Ashley retreated from Brightman and began to mumble. "Tricks, traps, trading time," said Ashley as she began to recite a poem that she had used to give herself strength. She had created the poem when she was a child to drive away the pain created by her abusive father.

Brightman remembered that line from the poem he had heard when he stood in the halls of time. His vision began to blur, and the white energy from his hands grew weaker.

"Tricks, traps, and trading time

Rhyme, rhyme, rhyme

Spend some time in the Dark!" cried Ashley.

"No!" screamed Brightman, falling to the ground.

A dark stained-glass memory panel filled a block in the bright light: a vision of an old man with long gray hair and white eyes sat in a wheelchair. The Black Mist hissed and jumped into the vision. Ashley disappeared from view, and Brightman fell into the black, surrounded by the sound of machinery.

Brightman's body stretched across a table unable to move. Drills and saws attached to long mechanical arms hovered in the air and glided toward him. The old man crawled toward Brightman slowly and deliberately. "Mr. B," said the soft voice of a little girl. "Mr. B."

"I did what you said," muttered Brightman. "I made my own memories."

"They aren't the right ones," said the little girl.

"He'll never figure it out," said a little boy. "He's not too bright for a Brightman."

"Mr. B," said the little girl, "You have to remember ... We have to go now, Mr. B. We can't stay. Our older selves are calling us back to them. You have to remember, Mr. B."

The voices of the children disappeared, replaced by the intrusive and menacing sounds of machinery. Brightman watched as his older self crawled closer and the blades approached his head. Images of the picture of his mother that Prinn had showed him flashed into his mind, and then the blackness began to fade.

Brightman appeared as a ghost within one of his earliest memories. He watched his mother play with him as a baby. Her warm smile filled his heart with comfort. The baby crawled on the floor, holding a stuffed crocodile. Two men entered the room and picked up the baby. Brightman's mother began crying as the men took him from her. John remembered her voice now from his first experiences within the Sub Blackness.

The men left the room, carrying Brightman's baby form away, but before disappearing, the baby dropped the small stuffed crocodile onto the floor. Brightman looked toward his mother and then picked up the stuffed animal. The memory faded, and he returned to the Sub Blackness. Brightman could move now. He held the stuffed animal and noticed a light begin to grow around it. The toy fell to the ground, slowly changing. A crocodile bigger than a truck appeared in the darkness. The animal whipped its tail and moved toward the old man on the ground. Its powerful jaws engulfed him and swallowed the older Brightman's frail body in two quick bites. Light surrounded the crocodile, and the beast exploded, filling the Sub Blackness with light.

Brightman woke up and saw Ashley passed out near his side. The sky began to change color to a bright white, and a black vortex opened. A large humanoid creature with deep red eyes, wings, and massive arms and legs appeared near the air base. The monstrosity towered into the sky, its size incomprehensible. "No!" boomed a loud unearthly voice. "No! I will destroy you all!"

The creature, its skin as black as midnight reflecting the sunlight, raised its massive arm. Muscles flexed, revealing the power of the creature. Its hand reached to the heavens and made a fist ready to strike the earth. Then a white chain extended from above and wrapped around the creature's massive arm. Another chain attached itself to the other arm and then the neck of the monstrosity. At the ends of the chain, enormous white female forms, larger than mountains, pulled back against Denod's strength. Long flowing white hair extended across the sky as slight but powerful arms with delicate hands and bony fingers reeled the chains in toward the heavens. Long robes flowed throughout the air as winds picked up cascading rays of light on the wasteland, bathing the area in the soft warmth of a comforting white aura.

"You cannot hide from us anymore, Denod!" boomed a voice, shaking the ground with its powerful tone.

Three dark figures atop massive steeds rode across the flowing robes. The shadowy muscular beings sent forth electricity from their clawlike hands into the chains. The energy flowed down the chains and wrapped around Denod's body. The electricity pulsated around Denod and began to flow through his muscles, constricting his movements and sapping his strength.

A large dark door appeared in front of Denod, and tiny red eyes began to spill out. The eyes swarmed in the air and surrounded Denod. Then light shot forth from within the eyes and dug into his black skin. Denod screamed in pain as the red eyes focused their gaze upon him. An eternity of torment and rage spilled forth from the eyes and attacked Denod. His body began to break apart and be absorbed into the dark door. The eyes continued to attack him with vengeful spite until his body scattered into millions of pieces, only to disappear into the darkness. The eyes blinked and hovered in the sky for a moment and then vanished.

During the commotion Bird slunk into the air base, carefully placed Leaf in a safe spot, and entered the room holding Marybeth. Bird looked upon the woman, who rose to her knees to stare back at Bird. "Well, well," said Marybeth, spitting out a bit of blood. "Looks like we are even. I took someone from you and you took someone from me."

Bird brandished her katana and stood in front of the woman. She turned her back to Marybeth and remained silent. In a quick and violent motion Bird twirled around and pushed her katana through Marybeth's skull. The blade cut through the woman's spine, the tip penetrating to the floor of the room. A stream of blood spewed from the woman's mouth, covering Bird's jumpsuit.

Marybeth stared into the distance, her dead eyes devoid of the madness that had infested them. Bird took off her helmet and tossed it to the ground. The blue-jay mold bounced and then settled by the corpse. Bird removed her jumpsuit and walked naked into the air base.

She picked up Leaf and left the building, wandering into the sea of flowers. Tears flowed from her eyes as her long blond hair flowed in the wind. Her hand reached down to touch the tall flowers that covered the ground. Bird held Leaf close and fell to her knees.

Brightman picked up Ashley and began to walk toward Bird. Prinn and Yanti joined him in the field of flowers. They started toward Bird, but Brightman put out his arm. A bright light formed near Bird, and celestial voices began to speak.

"It is time," said a female voice. "Your child does not belong in this world. He was born from the light of an Eternal. He cannot stay."

Bird looked into the light. "No," she cried. "Never. I will not part with my child."

"There is no other way," said the voice.

"Let her come with the child," said another voice.

"No, it violates the law."

"The law has already been violated. She has suffered enough. Denod's madness has caused enough pain. We are no better than him if we impart more."

"Fine."

"What about the Brightman?"

"What about him?"

"He possesses Learyana's gift. Are we sure we want to leave him here?"

"Maybe it's what this world needs to rebuild."

"Perhaps ..."

The light surrounding Bird and Leaf began to shine more brightly. Brightman watched as Bird stood up and walked forward. The image of a large grizzly bear and a fox followed. The light flashed, and she vanished with Leaf cradled in her arms.

* * * *

Ed and Lesly freed themselves from the armor and made their way over to the Speaker. Ed glared at him and poked him with his finger. "What are you going to do now?" he asked.

The Speaker looked at Ed and began to weep. His body started to writhe in the grasp of the vines. His skin became covered in boils, and pieces of flesh began rotting. The dead flesh slipped from bone and disappeared in the thick grass and vines that grew around his body. Ed backed away as the stages of Rot progressed through the Speaker at an unnatural pace. He and Lesly watched in horror as the man's body deteriorated in front of their eyes. A few of his followers in the area dropped their weapons and ran into the junglelike growth that spread for as far as the eye could see.

Ed and Lesly made their way back to the air base and met Yanti in the field that now occupied the open space in the area behind the base. They gathered around Ashley, who lay unconscious in a bed of tall flowers. Brightman held her hand and nervously looked at her unmoving body. Ashley opened her eyes and screamed, a small yarn figurine gripped tightly in her right hand. She flailed around and then began to calm down, accepting Brightman's embrace. Tears rolled down her cheeks and she closed her eyes. Annie ran up to Ashley and licked her hand. "Woof," said Annie.

The small group made their way back inside the air base, trying to grasp the events that had just played out in front of their eyes. Wonderment at what they had just observed stilled their tongues. A collective and agreed-upon silence followed the witnesses of the majesty that had unfurled across the wasteland.

VOICES FROM ABROAD

The group decided to bury Jessup's body amidst the field of flowers. Silence dominated the proceedings, and one by one members of the crew of misfits returned to the air base. Brightman sat with Ashley near the fireplace and comforted her as her memories, which she'd thought were erased by the mind wipes of the Elders, festered within her consciousness. Ed watched from the roof, keeping tabs on the remainder of the scattered cultists. Most wandered about the jungle growth, lost and aimless. Comfortable that the attackers posed no further threat, Ed joined the remainder of his allies in the main room. He sat with his friends. Each seemed lost in his or her own world, absorbing the chaos in a way that allowed them to understand what had happened. Ed glanced at the radio that sat in the corner. It remained silent.

Prinn cleared his throat and said, "I found this bottle of wine in Jessup's quarters. There was a note attached to it, saying, 'Saving this for the right time.' Unless someone feels this isn't the right time, I would like to open it."

Silence greeted Prinn's ears. "I'll take that as an okay, then."

Prinn took a knife out of his pocket and dug out the cork. "There might be a bit of the cork floating around in there. To Jessup and Bird and Leaf. Bless that child's soul." Prinn took a heavy sip and passed the bottle around. The group sat in silence, drinking the wine. Prinn skimmed through Bird's journal. Then he got up and walked around the room and looked at the kaleidoscope of pictures Jessup and Bird had pasted to the walls. He stopped for a moment at a postcard of the ocean, a palm tree, and a bird in the sky. *Curious*, he thought.

Brightman got up and walked over to the radio. He touched a knob, and a tiny white spark crackled from his finger. The radio began to play a slow comforting tune. He picked up the radio and noticed there were no batteries inside. He carefully placed it back down and took a sip of wine.

Yanti burst into the room. "Hey, guys, you need to listen to this!"

Tired eyes looked upon Yanti. "Seriously, you guys need to hear this."

The group slowly got up and followed Yanti to the tower, where they gathered around the radio transmitter. "I picked up this transmission a few minutes ago," said Yanti.

Yanti replayed the message. "Hello. Is anyone hearing me? Something is happening. We've got wild vegetation growing, and the creatures have been dropping over dead. Other reports are coming in about the oceans changing as well. Is anyone there?"

"Did you respond to the message, Yanti?" asked Brightman.

"No, not yet," said Yanti. "I wanted you to do it, Brightman. This message is coming from somewhere overseas. I can't pinpoint it yet, but it's definitely not close."

Yanti handed Brightman the microphone and clicked the button. Friends and family sat around Brightman, silently waiting for him to speak. "Hello."

ABOUT THE BOOK

Strange Events Even for an Apocalypse tells the tale of John Brightman. The story picks up after Ashley, a recon agent, frees Brightman from a biological prison. Ashley's mission, a simple one, is to return Brightman to the underground so the Elders can examine information recorded from a device implanted in his occipital lobe: vital secrets on how to defeat the creatures that attacked humanity years ago in a fight called the Flesh Wars.

Things don't go as planned, and Brightman must seek out unsuspecting allies in the apocalyptic wasteland. Guided by strange dreams and visions, Brightman discovers truths kept hidden for eons. The novel incorporates characters from *The Observer* and *A Breath Before Sunrise* as well as a host of new faces.

The ragtag group of unsuspecting friends must work together to defeat humanity's greatest threat. As mysteries begin to reveal themselves to Brightman, he must discover the means to defeat an enemy as old as time itself. Although humanity believed its greatest adversary attacked the very flesh and bone of life, a deeper and darker battle arises. In the stunning conclusion to *The Observer* and *A Breath Before Sunrise*, a climatic fight between light and darkness unfolds.

AUTHOR BIOGRAPHY

Jamie Horwath resides in northeastern Pennsylvania. He attended Penn State University during the nineties. After college he worked a series of odd jobs until taking a sales position for an employment agency. In 2011 Horwath released his first book, *Extinction Chronicles*, and since then has released five more. His work comprises short stories, novellas, and novelettes. His newest work is a novel completing the adventure that began as a short story titled *The Observer*.

Horwath's writing stays within the genres of science fiction, horror, and fantasy. His newest work crosses over all three categories. Jamie's dog, Storm, a beagle, is still hounding him.

Printed in the United States
By Bookmasters